The Little Buddha
Looking For Love

The Little Buddha
Looking For Love

Claus Mikosch

Illustrations by Kate Chesterton

AMMONITE
PRESS

This edition published 2019
by Ammonite Press
an imprint of Guild of Master Craftsman Publications Ltd
Castle Place, 166 High Street, Lewes,
East Sussex, BN7 1XU, United Kingdom
www.ammonitepress.com

First published by Verlag Herder

ISBN 978 1 78145 380 3

A catalogue record for this book is available from the British Library.

Publisher: Jason Hook
Design Manager: Robin Shields
Editor: Jamie Pumfrey

Colour reproduction by GMC Reprographics
Printed and bound in China

Contents

Chapter 1
Looking For Love

**P**owerful rays of sunlight touched his skin and a pleasant warmth spread through his body – from head to toe, from his fingertips all the way to his heart. He inhaled deeply and felt his surroundings awaken. After a long winter rest, nature was stretching its sleepy limbs. The branches were dancing in the wind, birds were singing and a wonderful scent filled the fresh air. The whole country was flourishing.

Two years had passed since the Little Buddha had returned from his first journey. He fondly remembered all the different experiences he'd had and the new friends he'd made, and sometimes he imagined what it would be like to travel the world again one day. Yet memories and dreams took up very little space in his day-to-day life – most of the time he was fully immersed in the present. He sat on the flat stone underneath his big old Bodhi tree and meditated almost every day and night; he dedicated his time to the inner stillness and observed the uniqueness of every moment with great passion.

*

The Little Buddha was happy with his life, happier than ever before in fact, because he wasn't constantly alone any more. Before, his old friend the farmer had been his only visitor, and he could only stop by on rare occasions. But then more and more strangers had started to appear under the Bodhi tree. They travelled from far away to ask him for advice – news had spread that the Little Buddha was able to help others find happiness. And indeed, with very few words he succeeded in making people feel better almost every time. He patiently listened to everyone and tried to put himself in their position. Often, he would tell one of the stories he had heard on his travels and was always delighted when the story put a smile on his visitor's face.

Despite his young age many called him a wise man and some even believed that he had special powers. But the Little Buddha didn't really understand what they meant; after all, he simply shared his experiences and his time with them. He didn't have a magic wand that would make their problems go away. Even so, hardly a week went by without someone coming to see him in search of happiness.

Until now he had always found a good answer to the many questions people brought to him. But then one day a man arrived who looked even sadder than all the others.

'Please, you must help me!'

The Little Buddha observed him carefully. The man was sitting in front of him with slouched shoulders and tears in his eyes.

'What's the matter?'

'I can't find a woman,' the man sobbed.

'But why do you need a woman?' the Little Buddha wondered.

'To experience true love. Without a woman that's not possible.'

'Are you sure? Because you can also love your parents or your neighbours, the birds or the trees.'

'Yes, but it's not the same. To love properly I need a woman.'

The man was totally disheartened.

'All of my friends are already married, all but me,' he complained. 'I also want to meet a woman, someone I can share my life with. I don't want to spend the rest of my days alone. Please, help me!'

The Little Buddha didn't know what to say. The whole love thing seemed to be much more complicated than he had thought.

'I'm afraid I don't know how to help you,' he said after a while. 'I haven't had any experience with women and true love yet.'

'But there must be something you can do. I beg you!'

The man sounded desperate. The Little Buddha felt pity for the man but how was he able to help him without really understanding the problem himself? How could he offer advice about love when he wasn't exactly sure what true love is?

They sat in silence for some time. Then the Little Buddha had an idea.

'Maybe there is something I can do.'

A glimmer of hope appeared on the man's face.

'But you will have to wait for your answer for a few months.'

'A few months? Why so long?'

'Because, first, I myself need to learn about true love.'

The Little Buddha had become curious. And there was only one way to satisfy his curiosity: he had to set out and ask life in person! He wanted to discover the meaning of true love not just for his visitor, but for himself too. And he hoped he would learn how to find it.

*

The very next morning he packed his bag with some food and a warm blanket and said goodbye to the big old Bodhi tree. He closed his eyes, took a deep breath and embarked on a journey for the second time in his life.

It was spring – the perfect time for a new beginning.

Looking For Love

Chapter 2
The Yearning Postman

he path ran through meadows and open fields. Every now and then a little hill and a few trees appeared in the distance but otherwise there was just blue sky as far as the eye could see. The landscape was mundane in some ways, yet at the same time it was very beautiful.

If one took the time to look closely there were little treasures to be discovered everywhere: the first flowers timidly raising their heads from the earth to make sure winter was really over; wild rabbits joyfully chasing each other through the fields; or tiny snails who travelled so slowly it seemed they'd never get anywhere. Perhaps they weren't even looking to get anywhere.

The Little Buddha had set off without a clear direction in mind. He went with the flow and felt as free as the clouds that had accompanied him during the first hours of his journey. He had seen them drifting by high up in the sky – now they had disappeared, and he wondered where they had gone to.

*

Late in the morning he reached a crossroads. He had already passed by here the last time he had gone on a journey. The road straight ahead led to the big city but this time he didn't want to go there. He stopped for a moment and looked around. While contemplating which direction to choose he saw a colourful butterfly fluttering by. The butterfly was heading south – maybe that was a sign? Or maybe not. Or was it? It didn't matter. The Little Buddha decided to head south and turned right.

He marched towards the sun for the rest of the day. Twice he took a break to eat and meditate but both times he only stopped for a short while. Even though it had been a long time since he had walked so much, he wasn't tired at all. The movement seemed to give him extra energy so why should he take long breaks? He continued with a steady breath, enjoying every single step.

*

When it began to get dark, he climbed up a little hill to see where he could spend the night. Not far from the hill, in a narrow valley, he spotted a house – surely he would find shelter there, he thought confidently. He climbed down the hill in the last of the daylight and soon found himself standing in front of a big wooden building.

The Little Buddha stepped onto the porch and knocked on the door. Nothing. He tried again but still there was no answer. Suddenly, he heard a galloping horse approaching behind him. He turned around and could make out the silhouette of a rider in the twilight. A middle-aged man jumped off the saddle, tied the horse to a pole and came towards his visitor.

'Good evening!'

'Good evening!' the Little Buddha replied.

'Can I help you?'

'I'm a traveller and I'm looking for a place to spend the night.'

'And you thought I might have space for you?'

The man gave the Little Buddha a suspicious look.

'Yes, that's what I was hoping for. But if not it's no problem, I can look somewhere else.'

'And your horse?' the man asked.

'I don't have a horse.'

'So how would you find a different shelter? It takes almost two hours to get to the next house.'

'I could sleep under a tree like I usually do.'

The man eyed him sceptically again but then his serious frown turned into a friendly smile.

'Of course you can stay here! Many people visit me, there's even a spare room.'

'Thank you, that's so kind!'

The man smiled and looked the Little Buddha up and down.

'Is it possible we've met before?'

The Little Buddha thought for a moment, then he remembered.

'That's right, you're the postman!'

A few years ago, the postman had delivered him a letter but in the darkness he hadn't recognized his face straight away. The postman returned to his horse and grabbed a big, tightly packed bag.

'Are these all letters?'

'Yes.'

'There must be loads of them,' the Buddha marvelled.

'There sure are. People have lots of things to say to each other.'

The postman lit an oil lamp, unlocked the door and together they stepped into the house. The first thing the Little Buddha caught sight of was an old armchair next to the entrance. It looked incredibly comfortable.

'Do you want a cup of tea?' the postman asked.

'That would be great, thank you!'

'Good. Make yourself at home, I'll be right back.'

*

While the postman disappeared into the kitchen, the Little Buddha let himself sink into the armchair. It was a great relief to finally sit down after a long day's march. For a few moments he closed his eyes and joyfully observed how his whole body relaxed. But soon his curiosity arose, and he began to look around the room.

There were two more armchairs, a small cupboard, a shelf holding lots of books and a big desk. In the corner next to him was a chimney and in front of him a low table. On the wall behind the desk he saw a large map and two windows reflected the dim light of the lamp. He was just beginning to inspect the map more closely when the postman returned with hot, steaming tea.

They both took a careful sip of their drinks, then the postman put down his cup, emptied the bag on the desk and began to sort the letters into different piles.

'How long have you been a postman for?' the Little Buddha asked.

'All my life. My father was a postman too – when I was young, I often helped him here in the office and sometimes I even joined him on the delivery tours.'

'And what's the life of a postman like?'

'I can't complain really. It's a lot of work and I always have to go out, even when it's raining and storming. But I meet lots of people and most of them are happy to see me.'

The two men smiled. It's a good feeling to be welcomed.

'Do you have to go to all the places on the map?' the Little Buddha asked.

The postman nodded and began to explain: he was responsible for a whole province, in total eleven villages – the furthest was half a day's ride away. Once a week he visited every village, took the mail to the residents and picked up the letters that were destined for other villages or faraway cities. In the evenings he would sort the mail that had to be delivered the following days. All the mail for other provinces was picked up by the stagecoach twice a week, leaving him with everything from other areas he then had to take charge of.

He knew almost every person in the province, some had even become his friends. Every day, he would be filled in on all the important and unimportant news and sometimes people would invite him in for lunch or a cup of tea. If someone lived alone and wasn't able to read, he took the time to read the letters aloud to them. Often, he would also write the responses, because those who couldn't read weren't able to write either. If bad news came in the mail, he'd give the sad recipient a hug, if the news was good, he shared their joy. Occasionally the news he delivered was so good, the recipients would give him fruit and cakes. Once a hunter who had just learned he had become a grandfather gave the postman a whole wild boar.

As the postman talked about his work the Little Buddha began to feel very tired. The first day of his journey had been much harder than he had realized. He really wanted to keep listening, but the postman's words became more and more fuzzy. Before long, he had fallen asleep in the armchair.

*

He woke up in the middle of the night. The oil lamp had gone out, but the room wasn't completely dark. The Little Buddha looked up to find the postman sitting at his desk, writing a letter by candlelight. The Little Buddha remained quiet in his armchair for a while, watching his host.

Carefully he interrupted the silence.

'Who are you writing to so late at night?'

The postman was startled, after all he had thought his guest was fast asleep.

'It's a letter to a woman.'

'Your wife?' the Little Buddha asked.

The postman shook his head.

'Don't you have a wife?'

'No. Unfortunately I haven't found the right woman yet. But I'm looking for her – that's why I sit here and write.'

The Little Buddha pondered this for a moment.

'Do you want to marry the woman you're writing to?'

The postman shook his head once more.

'The last two letters from her weren't very exciting. This is the last time I am going to write to her. But luckily there are plenty of others on my list.'

'What list?'

The postman hesitated, then shrugged his shoulders and looked the Little Buddha in the eyes.

'I'm looking for the perfect woman! As a postman I know almost all the women in the area so I made a list of all the suitable ones. And whenever I meet a woman I don't know yet and who I think is pretty – one who is not too old and not too young, not too big and not too skinny –I add her to the list as well.'

'And then?'

'Little by little I work through my list by exchanging letters with them. But never with several women at the same time, always just with one. By writing letters, I get to know her and find out if she is a good fit for me.'

'And if she's a good fit?'

'That hasn't happened yet,' the postman sighed. 'There's always something that bothers me.'

'Like what?'

'That depends. Some are too serious, others too childish; some talk too much, others too little; some are boring, and some are too crazy.'

They fell silent for a moment.

'Have you written to many women?'

The postman got up, went to the cupboard and opened a drawer overflowing with letters.

'These are just the replies I got during the last year. As you can see, I'm quite busy – I hardly have time for anything else in the evenings,' he complained. 'It's not easy to find true love.'

There it was again, love.

'So, what do you expect from the perfect woman?' the Little Buddha asked.

Now it was the postman who had to ponder.

'I simply wish,' he said after a while, 'I'd find a woman with whom I can have a harmonious relationship. Most married people I know constantly argue with their partners. I don't want that. I want to be always happy.'

Once more silence conquered the room. The Little Buddha wondered whether it was actually possible to always be happy. And was it necessary?

'When you argue with someone you can also make up afterwards, can't you? And perhaps you can learn something from the argument.'

'That's true. But wouldn't it be much better to learn without arguing? And I think the only way that's possible is if you first make sure you are well suited to one another.'

'But are you sure that exchanging letters is enough to find out who is the best match for you? Some women might suit you much better when you get to know them in person rather than only on paper. Maybe you should meet up with them, at least sometimes.'

'Um...'

The postman frowned, even though he liked the idea. If it would help him find the right partner, why not?

'And what will happen if you don't find the perfect woman?' the Little Buddha asked after a short pause.

'Don't say something like that! If I keep on looking, I will definitely find her. She has to be somewhere, after all there's a perfect partner for everyone, isn't there?'

The Little Buddha shrugged his shoulders. He had never thought about this. But he doubted the possibility of two people being made for one another. People were simply too different. Besides, he thought it was a little strange that someone would spend so much time searching. If the perfect woman really existed, surely she'd appear all by herself at some point?

'Have you ever tried to stop looking and simply wait?'

'I'm not patient enough. Plus, I'm not that young and eventually I'd like to have a family too.'

'But perhaps you're searching so much you're not leaving enough space in your life to actually find the right woman.'

The postman looked at him in disbelief as if he thought the Little Buddha was too young to understand.

'I think we had better go to bed, it's already late and I have a long day ahead of me tomorrow,' the postman said. He showed his visitor the guest room, said good night and blew out the candle.

The Little Buddha lay down and his eyes immediately began to close.

Just before he fell asleep, he had a final thought: maybe it isn't a bad thing to keep searching and chase your dreams – just as long as the yearning doesn't prevent you from enjoying what you already have.

Chapter 3
The Woodcutter's Wife

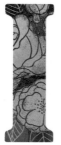I n the morning, the Little Buddha and the postman had breakfast and shared stories about their lives. Afterwards the postman started to prepare for his work day. He tied the different piles of letters together with string, put them in two big bags and packed everything onto the horse.

'Shall I give you a ride?'

The Little Buddha glanced at the waiting animal sceptically. It seemed friendly but at the same time it also commanded his respect. He had never ridden a horse before.

'Is there enough space for both of us?'

'Of course. You just sit behind me.'

'I'm not sure...'

'Didn't you tell me you enjoy trying new things?'

'Yes, I guess you're right.'

The postman helped him onto the horse's back, then climbed onto the saddle himself and took the reins.

'Hold tight!'

As the Little Buddha wondered why he had to hold tight, the journey began. Not in a mellow trot as he had hoped but at a fierce gallop. The postman seemed to be in a hurry.

'Watch out, tree trunk!'

'What?' the Little Buddha yelled, but he didn't get an answer. Instead the horse made a big leap and jumped over a fallen tree blocking the path. The Little Buddha nearly fell off. He clung to the body in front of him and squinted his eyes. But the next problem presented itself right away: he was starting to feel nauseous! If he had known what was awaiting him, he wouldn't have eaten so much breakfast but now it was too late. He quickly opened his eyes again and tried to concentrate on his breath. Deep inside he prayed there wouldn't be too many obstacles along the way.

The wild ride lasted for half an hour, then the postman suddenly pulled the reins, the horse came to a stop and the Little Buddha sighed with great relief.

The postman jumped off, rummaged through one of the bags and headed towards an old stone house in the middle of the countryside. The Little Buddha got off too. He was glad to tread on solid ground again. Soon after, the postman returned.

'Let's go!'

But the Little Buddha hesitated.

'To be honest I'd rather walk. I prefer to travel at a slower pace.'

He thanked the postman for his hospitality and they said their goodbyes. Less than a minute later the postman had disappeared behind a huge cloud of dust and the Little Buddha was by himself again.

The path led south. He continued walking straight ahead, placing one foot after the other and enjoying the fresh spring air. He trusted life to give him exactly the experiences he needed in order to find answers to his questions. The direction would present itself. And even if his questions remained unanswered, every experience and every encounter would provide a valuable lesson.

*

When the sun had reached its highest point, a cart pulled by two donkeys came towards the Little Buddha. The back of the cart was piled with wood and the donkeys breathed heavily under the great weight they were pulling. A slender woman sat at the front of the cart, spurring the animals on with the whip in her hand. The Little Buddha stepped aside, greeted the woman and watched the cart pass by. 'Poor donkeys,' he thought compassionately. Then he focused again on the path and continued his journey.

*

Two hours later he was just about to take a break when the donkey cart caught up with him, this time heading in the same direction as him. The cart rolled up next to him and the woman made the donkeys come to a halt.

'Would you like to hop on?' she offered, giving him a friendly look.

The Little Buddha didn't have to think twice and smiled gratefully. He climbed onto the narrow seat of the cart and sat down next to the woman. The donkeys started to pull and the cart rolled on.

The Little Buddha noticed that the wood was missing from the back. He was happy the cart was much lighter now, so the donkeys didn't have to work as hard.

'Where did you take all the logs?' he asked.

'To a buyer who is building a house. My husband is a woodcutter and works in the forest all day. I'm the one who has to deliver the wood.'

'All by yourself?'

'Yes, but the loading and unloading is done by others. I just drive the cart.'

'And now? Are you going home?'

The woman nodded and cracked her whip in the air to keep the donkeys moving.

'When I get back, I'll have to feed these two lazybones and then

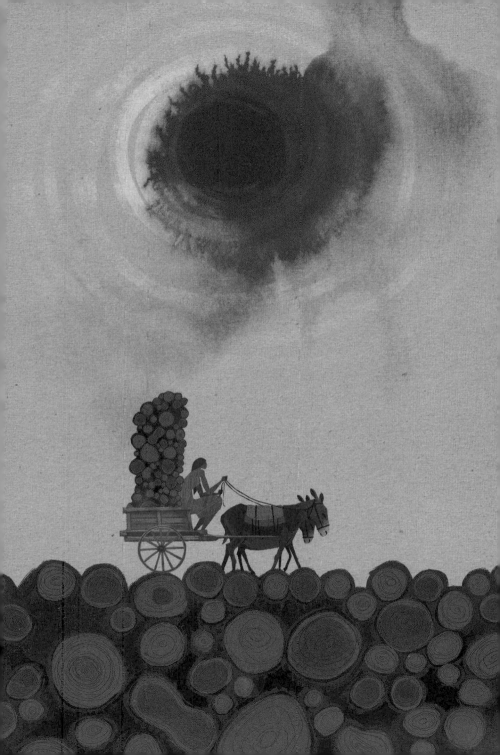

I have to cook. When my husband returns from work, he's always very hungry. And I also have to pick my children up from their grandparents' house.'

'How many children do you have?'

'Five.'

'Five!' the Little Buddha replied, astonished. 'You don't look that old.'

'I'm not, I just started early,' she winked at him. 'What about you? What are you doing and where are you heading to?'

The Little Buddha began to tell her about his life, how he spent most of his time meditating under his Bodhi tree and about this being his second journey. He explained that he didn't have any exact plans, instead he preferred to be surprised by each day. The woman listened to him with great interest. When he had finished talking the Little Buddha noticed a longing, almost sad expression on the woman's face.

'Aren't you happy?' he asked carefully.

She shrugged her shoulders as if she didn't have an answer to his question.

'You know, I have to work every day, from dawn to dusk, and that's very tiring.'

'Can't you take holidays every now and then?'

The woman laughed.

'No. We have to earn money to pay for our house and to be able to put enough food on the table for everyone.'

The Little Buddha smiled at her sympathetically. Then another thought came to him.

'But, surely, it's also nice to have a big family, isn't it?'

'Yes, indeed. Though sometimes I wish I could travel around and roam freely. Just like you.'

For a while they rolled on in silence. As they continued to ride along the path, the Little Buddha pondered her words.

'If you don't mind me asking, why did you have five children so quickly? You could have waited a bit and would have had time to travel.'

'That probably would have been better... But I had been dreaming about a romantic wedding since I was a young child. I desperately wanted to get married, to wear a beautiful dress and to be a real princess for a day. I wanted to feel in safe hands and have my own family.'

'And you've succeeded, haven't you?'

'Yes, but I thought that I'd be happy forever if I achieved all of this. Reality is different though to the life I'd painted in my fantasy.'

It was the third time within just a few days the Little Buddha had heard about the desire for eternal happiness. First the man who had visited him under his tree, then the yearning postman and now the woodcutter's wife. They all spoke of finding a way to defeat sadness once and for all. But just as the bright day and the dark night belong to each other, happiness and sadness are perhaps inseparable too. If you want one you also have to welcome the other.

'I've accepted my situation,' the woman continued, 'and I know that you can't have everything. A big family and travelling the world are simply two very different things.'

'But would you exchange your children for a journey?'

'No, of course not. But I definitely wouldn't get married that quickly again. I think it's much better to have some time for yourself first. And before entering a marriage you should also carefully consider whether you really want to spend the rest of your life with that person.'

'But some problems will always arise, won't they? No matter who you're with.'

The Little Buddha told her about his encounter with the postman and his desperate search for the perfect woman.

'The poor soul,' the woodcutter's wife replied compassionately. 'I guess he will be looking forever. No, the perfect partner doesn't exist. If you want to avoid problems, I'm afraid marriage is not for you.'

'So, what is important to make it work?'

'Quite a lot! Marriage always means plenty of work. After all there are not only highs but also many lows – sometimes even love is in a bad mood! You have to help each other deal with everyday life, and most importantly you have to be honest with each other.'

The path steepened and the cart moved on slowly. The woman had to use the whip several times to avoid rolling back down the hill. The donkeys wheezed loudly but they soon reached the top.

'I think when it's true love you will find a solution for every problem.'

'And how do you know that it's true love?' the Little Buddha asked.

The woman paused for a moment before she answered.

'True love means that you accept the other person without trying to change them.'

The Little Buddha smiled and let the woman's words sink in.

'And how is it with you and your husband? Is it true love?'

Again there was silence, this time a bit longer.

'I wish it were but if I'm honest, no. We are a family and we get on well, but nothing more. We respect each other but, unfortunately, we are too different. The shared dreams that make life exciting are missing. I would love to live by the sea one day, but my husband is not interested at all. I love dancing, he doesn't; I enjoy being with people while my husband prefers to be alone in the forest. There are many things that I miss.'

'And what do you miss most?'

'Affection! You know, for most men love is just a fairy tale – good for poems, songs and romantic stories but totally useless in real life. He always thinks I expect him to worship me and to give me huge gifts. But that's not true. It's the little things that make the difference: some flowers, a few nice words, a hug. You don't have to give someone diamonds to show them love.'

The woman turned to the Little Buddha.

'You might not believe it, but my husband has never ever brought me flowers, even though he passes a big hedge of roses every day.'

'Oh, I'm sorry.'

'Don't worry. I've got used to it by now.'

The Little Buddha tried to find a way to help her.

'Have you ever told your husband what you're missing?'

'No. I think he should work it out for himself.'

'But you said you are very different. How should he know what you want?'

For a while the woman was in deep thought and stared straight ahead. Then she turned back to the Little Buddha and smiled.

'Thank you for your advice, I will try to talk to him. Who knows, perhaps it really is possible for me to become happier. Our marriage definitely deserves a chance.'

*

Late in the afternoon they reached a crossroads where the woman turned off to go home. The Little Buddha climbed off the cart, waved goodbye to the woman and continued alone. As he walked on, he wondered whether her desires would be fulfilled one day. Of course, the best thing would be if the relationship with her husband changed for the better and they'd be happy together. If not, she would probably have to be patient and wait until her children were old enough to look after themselves. Maybe then she'd meet a man who was better suited for her. Someone who would like to dance with her, who would travel with her to the sea and bring her flowers after work.

The Woodcutter's Wife
35

Chapter 4
The Jealous
Castle Owner

fter saying goodbye to the woodcutter's wife, the Little Buddha focused on walking again. In the distance he saw the outskirts of a big forest – maybe it was the same forest he had crossed during his first journey? He wasn't sure though because there were many forests in the country and if you didn't know them well they were difficult to distinguish from one another.

The sun was slowly setting and dark clouds had appeared. There was no house to be seen anywhere, so the Little Buddha started to look for shelter. Normally he would have slept under a tree but none of the trees around him had enough leaves to protect him from the approaching rain. Luckily he discovered a small ledge underneath a big rock not far from the path, just as the first drops hit the ground. The Little Buddha found just enough space and made himself comfortable while the rain poured down. He wrapped the blanket around him, ate some of the food and thought about the same question he always pondered when it was raining heavily: how was it possible for a few clouds to carry that much water?

*

The next morning the Little Buddha woke up early. The sun had just risen and the first warm rays welcomed him after a good night's rest. He put the blanket back into the bag and continued his journey – a new day was waiting to be lived.

The Little Buddha had already been walking for a few hours when he reached an area that seemed strangely familiar. While trying to remember where he was, he heard dogs barking in the distance. Shortly afterwards the path made a sharp right turn and suddenly he knew where he was: just a few hundred metres away stood the castle with the beautiful garden in which he had spent some time on his first journey. Did his friend the gardener still work there, he wondered. 'I'm sure he does,' he thought, 'where else would he be?' The Little Buddha felt his heart beating faster. He almost started running but then paused to do exactly the opposite – he walked more slowly so he could enjoy the wonderful feeling of anticipation for as long as possible.

*

When he set foot on the huge estate, the Little Buddha was immediately greeted by the two castle dogs, who obviously hadn't forgotten him. He was happy to see them, too.

Everything was still very familiar to him, especially the small path that led directly to the gardener's cottage. He knocked on the door but didn't get an answer. After a few more unsuccessful attempts he went to the vegetable garden on the other side of the cottage. He looked around but there was no sign of his friend. 'He's probably in the village doing some shopping,' he thought. So, the Little Buddha sat down on a step and waited patiently.

After an hour the gardener still hadn't shown up. It wouldn't have been a problem if the Little Buddha hadn't been overcome by great hunger. When he spent the whole day sitting under his Bodhi tree, he hardly needed any food. But it was very different when he was on the road all day. His stomach rumbled so loudly it was almost impossible for him to meditate peacefully. He checked his bag, but he had already eaten the last of his provisions the previous evening. He couldn't find anything edible in the garden either because the plants were only just starting to blossom and weren't carrying any fruit yet. Besides, he wanted a warm meal. He weighed his options: maybe he'd get some food in the castle.

Accompanied by the two dogs, he followed the path back to the main entrance until he found himself standing in front of a big wooden door. It was only a small castle, without tower and ditch, but nevertheless it was a real castle. The gardener had told him once that a prince had lived here many years ago. The Little Buddha grabbed the heavy iron ring that was attached to the door and banged it against the wood. Just a few seconds later the door opened with a loud creak. An older man with uncombed hair and a thick beard looked down at him grumpily – it was the castle owner himself.

'What do you want?'

'Sorry to disturb you,' the Little Buddha replied politely, 'I'm here because I want to visit my friend, the gardener, but he's not home yet. I've been travelling for more than two days and I'm really hungry, so I was wondering whether you might have something for me to eat.'

'Weren't you here a few years ago?'

'Yes!' the Little Buddha nodded. He was glad the man remembered him.

'Alright then,' grumbled the castle owner, 'come in. You're lucky, I was just about to have lunch anyway. Some soup and bread, that's all there is.'

'Great, that's enough for me.'

The Little Buddha followed the man into the dark entrance hall. A long gloomy corridor led them to the dining room.

'Take a seat, I'll be right back.'

*

While the castle owner disappeared into the kitchen, the Little Buddha sat down at the table and looked around. Right next to him, brown curtains covered most of the window so only very little light entered from outside. However, the curtains weren't the only reason the room was dark: it was also hopelessly overcrowded. Books, colourful glasses and little statues were piled up on shelves; decorated plates and dusty oil paintings in golden frames covered the walls; there were locked chests on the floor and a huge chandelier with burnt-down candles dangled from the ceiling. The Little Buddha had never seen so many things in a single room! It lacked love, though. The whole building was cold and dark, and the dining room felt terribly uncomfortable. He was grateful the man had opened the door to him, but he didn't feel very welcome.

*

Suddenly he heard the sound of rattling crockery from the kitchen.

'Damn!' he heard the castle owner swearing.

Shortly afterwards the man returned and handed him a bowl of soup. He couldn't set it down, though, because the table was overcrowded with all sorts of stuff.

'Did anything break?' the Little Buddha enquired.

'It would be better to ask what hasn't broken yet. Two weeks ago, my servant ran away and since then the kitchen has turned into a battlefield.'

'Why has he run away?'

'Because... ' the castle owner began, but quickly fell silent again. 'Wait, I've forgotten something. I have to do everything myself, it really is appalling!'

He got up with a sigh, shuffled to the kitchen and came back with a few slices of bread. He sat down and hastily began to gulp up the hot soup. When his bowl was half empty, he paused.

'I don't really know why my servant has gone. He said he couldn't stand it here any longer even though I've always paid him generously.'

'Perhaps it was too dark for him here,' his visitor suggested tentatively.

'Do you think it's too dark here?'

The Little Buddha nodded while scooping in another mouthful of soup.

'The thing is,' the castle owner explained, 'too much light damages the books and the paintings. They'd lose value and I can't allow that to happen.'

'Why do you have so much stuff in the first place?' the Little Buddha asked him.

'Because I'm a collector. I collect everything that's valuable. There are fifteen rooms in my castle and every room is packed with precious items. I also own quite a lot of silver and gold. It has taken me many years to gather all these riches.'

'And what do you do with it all?'

'Nothing. I wait. My wealth increases in value with time and so I only get richer and richer,' the castle owner responded proudly. His eyes were twinkling with greed.

The Little Buddha didn't know what to say. He was convinced that too many possessions made life unnecessarily heavy instead of making it lighter. Most of all he couldn't understand why someone would want to have so many things he couldn't actually use.

'I collect something too,' he finally said.

'Oh yes, what?'

'Special moments.'

'But that's not the same,' the castle owner replied. 'You can only collect things that you can sell for more money later on.'

'I can't sell them, that's true. But collecting moments has a big advantage over collecting things: moments can't be stolen!'

Now it was the castle owner who was speechless.

For a while they remained quiet and focused on lunch. When they had finished eating, the host took the bowls to the kitchen.

*

The Little Buddha continued to look around the room. His attention was drawn to a painting that showed the castle owner with his family. When the man returned with a pot of tea, the Little Buddha decided to ask him about them.

'Where are your children? I remember them well, I often played with them in the garden on my last visit.'

'They ran away last week too,' the man sighed. 'With my wife.'

'Why?' the Little Buddha asked, slightly shocked.

'They also said that they couldn't stand it here any longer. Well, my wife did but since she has always looked after our children, she has taken them with her.'

'But didn't your wife explain why she didn't want to stay with you?'

'Yes, she did...'

Silence filled the room while the castle owner tried to hide behind his cup of tea. He would have preferred to end the conversation there and then.

'Doesn't she love you any more?'

'It's not that. She said she won't come back until I've changed.'

'What does she want you to change?'

'My jealousy.'

'And is it true that you're jealous?'

'Maybe.'

'Maybe?'

The Little Buddha had to extract every single word from him.

'What happened?'

'I banned her from leaving the castle grounds.'

'Why?'

'Because she went to the village several times a week. I didn't want that.'

'And why didn't you want that?'

Again there was silence for a few moments.

'I was worried she might be meeting another man. Every time she left, I got angry. I wanted all her attention for me only. Why should she go out all the time, when she has everything she needs right here?'

'Perhaps she wanted to meet some friends.'

'Yes, she told me the same thing but I didn't believe her. She accused me of not giving any love, of only wanting to receive. But I do love her...'

By now the Little Buddha pitied him. Of course, he understood the woman – she didn't want to be told what to do and had every right to pack her things and leave. But the castle owner wanted to be loved, just like everyone else. Sadly, he hadn't realized that no one should be forced to give up everything for the other person. By trying to keep love captive, he had chased it away. He was still rich but there was no one left to share his riches with.

'I don't understand why I can't own love just like I own a painting or a castle,' the man said.

'But how can you own something that you can't hold on to?'

The Little Buddha didn't get an answer to this question. Perhaps the castle owner knew deep inside that he could neither buy nor own love, but he didn't want to accept it. He was used to getting everything he wanted. And he was probably scared to lose what he had, regardless of whether it was a castle or love.

Chapter 5
The Worried Student

I n the early afternoon the Little Buddha left the dark castle and returned to the cottage to see whether the gardener had come home. He knocked a couple of times and immediately heard footsteps coming from inside. The door opened, and the gardener stood before him. A happy smile spread out over his face and he greeted the Little Buddha with a heartfelt hug.

'What a nice surprise!'

Two years had passed since they had last seen each other. The gardener had some work to do in the vegetable beds, and the Little Buddha joined him so they could talk about everything they had experienced.

Once they'd brought each other up to date, the Little Buddha told him about his strange encounter with the castle owner.

'It doesn't surprise me at all that his wife has left him and taken the children,' the gardener said. 'Imagine seeing a beautiful bird and putting it in a cage to stop it from flying away so you can stare at it all the time. It wouldn't take long for the bird to become sad and lose a big part of its beauty. No, love doesn't work like that – if you try to own it, you kill it! Love shouldn't be locked away, it has to be free if you want to admire it.'

'So why do you think the castle owner wants to own everything?' the Little Buddha asked, as he kneeled down to help the gardener pull out the weeds.

'Because he feels insecure. He hopes his wealth will take away the fear of being alone and unprotected in the world. It's the same with his wife, he's not looking for love but security! Unfortunately, he hasn't understood that the desire for security will disappear once you start loving truthfully.'

'Instead he got jealous...'

'Yes. And you know the reason for jealousy?'

The Little Buddha shook his head.

'Jealousy starts when you spend too much time thinking about the future. You assume that something bad will happen even though it's impossible to know what will happen. You end up worrying and holding on to these anxious thoughts. I know a good story about this, do you want to hear it?'

The Little Buddha nodded joyfully, he hadn't heard a new story for quite some time. So they let the weeds be weeds for a while and sat down on a big rock next to the vegetable bed. Then the gardener began to tell the story.

*

A master and his student were returning to their temple after a pilgrimage. Around midday they arrived at a river they had to cross. An old woman was standing by the riverbank, desperately trying to figure out how to get to the other side. There was no bridge and she was afraid of the strong current. Without a second thought, the master offered to help. The woman gratefully accepted his offer and he carried her across the river on his back. He put the woman down on the other side and they continued on their separate ways. The student had followed his master across the river and had watched with horror how he had carried the woman. Their religion strictly prohibited them from touching women. As they walked towards the temple, the student kept thinking about the master's sin. How could he have dared to carry the woman on his back? Surely God would punish him for this. And what if the student was punished too? After all, he hadn't done anything to prevent his master from this dishonourable deed. He spent the whole afternoon greatly worried about what would happen to them now.

Just before they reached the temple, he couldn't bear it any longer and told the master about his worries.

'How could you carry the woman across the river? You know very well that we are not allowed to touch women.'

The master stayed calm and kept walking. He had noticed his student had been dwelling on what had happened at the river. Finally, he broke his silence:

'You are right, I touched the woman and carried her across the river, even though we shouldn't touch women. But I let go of her straight away. You are the one who has been carrying her in his thoughts ever since.'

*

Just as on his last visit, the Little Buddha stayed with the gardener for several weeks. During the day he helped him in the garden; he planted new seeds and seedlings, watered the lawn and bushes, cleared the beds of the steadily growing weeds and dug up the soil. He really loved the work because the garden was one of the best places to enjoy spring. Colourful flowers and fruits grew everywhere, the trees bore new leaves and an endless number of insects danced under the sun. Everything was in motion and the constant change of life was visible all around. The Little Buddha thought a person like the castle owner would benefit greatly from spending more time in the garden, he'd see the impermanence of everything with his own eyes and would come to understand that it doesn't make sense to hold on to anything. Instead of fearfully looking to the future, he'd learn to embrace the present wholeheartedly.

In the evenings the Little Buddha and the gardener sat in front of the open fire for many hours, drinking tea made with fresh herbs and philosophizing about life. Occasionally they meditated together and immersed themselves in the deep silence that surrounded them. No wonder the Little Buddha totally forgot about the time and didn't notice as the days flew by.

The gardener spoke about the mountains with great enthusiasm. Since the Little Buddha had never been in a proper mountain range, the thought of ending his stay in the castle garden and continuing his journey started sounding more and more attractive. Then, almost one month after his arrival, the time had finally come: he wanted to head north to the place where the high peaks touched the sky.

*

On their last night, the gardener lit a little fire outside the cottage. The Little Buddha had already shared many things from his travels but that night he mainly spoke about all the different people he had met – the sad man who had visited him under his tree, the yearning postman, the woodcutter's wife and, of course, the jealous castle owner.

'They all speak about love but none of them are really happy. Maybe they would feel better if they tried to look for happiness elsewhere? I agree that it's important to find love but does it have to be with one particular person?'

'I know what you mean,' the gardener replied, 'and you're right, love shouldn't be limited to one person only. But I think there's something else that people miss, something that has to do with love but can't be compared to the love you feel for a friend or an animal or a flower.'

The Little Buddha gave him a curious look. What could that be?

'It's the yearning to be in love.'

For a moment, only the crackling of the fire could be heard.

'The problem starts once you try the sweet fruit for the first time. Once you've been properly in love you will always feel the desire to have that amazing experience again.'

The gardener noticed that the Little Buddha couldn't quite follow his words.

'What about you? Have you ever been in love?'

'No, I don't think so,' the Little Buddha answered, shaking his head.

'Really? You've never had butterflies in your stomach?'

'Butterflies? In my stomach?' The Little Buddha was confused.

'Yes, that's how you say it. It's difficult to describe this feeling. You're overwhelmed with happiness and you feel like hugging the whole world. Everything seems wonderful and it's as if you and the other person become one. I fully understand why people miss being in love when they haven't experienced it for quite a while.'

'And how do you do that? Fall in love?'

'Well, unfortunately it's not that easy. Or perhaps it's easy but it's not a conscious decision. You can't plan it – usually it happens when you least expect it. Someone appears in your life and all of a sudden you feel a tingling, right here.'

He pointed to the area around his navel.

'That's why you call it "having butterflies" when you refer to being in love. Because it feels as though hundreds of butterflies are flying around in your stomach. Believe me, it's a very unique and overwhelming sensation.'

The Little Buddha grew more and more curious. He really wanted to experience this unknown feeling himself.

'What about you? Have you been in love too?' he asked his friend.

'Yes,' was the reply, 'and I hope that one day I will fall in love again.'

'So what happened the last time? Did the butterflies escape?'

The gardener had to laugh.

'You could put it that way, yes. You know, being in love is so incredibly intense it's almost impossible to maintain that feeling. Like everything else in life, love constantly changes too. That's why you shouldn't hold on to being in love. If you're lucky some butterflies stay inside and it's possible they might multiply again at some point. Sometimes they all fly away though.'

'That's a pity,' the Little Buddha said. 'But then surely they fly somewhere else.'

'Yes, that's what they do. And if you let go of the old butterflies there's a good chance that new ones will land in your stomach eventually.'

They smiled and sat by the fire in silence for a while. When the time came to go to bed, the gardener turned to the Little Buddha once more.

'Love has many different faces. Being in love is just one of them. If you ask me, the most important thing is to be patient because...'

He paused for a moment before finishing the sentence.

'Because patience means to love time.'

Chapter 6
The Hard-working Weaver

he next morning the Little Buddha said goodbye to the gardener and gave him a long hug. Then he set off and headed north. The mountains were several days away, lots of travelling was ahead of him.

The first hours he spent walking along the same route on which he had come. On his right was the big forest and in front of him the path wound through a hilly landscape. Around midday he left the hills and the forest behind and followed the path along the open fields. When it got dark the Little Buddha started to look out for a house or at least a tree, but far and wide there was nothing to be seen. He had no choice but to take his blanket and make himself comfortable in the fields.

*

The night was cold and clear. He stared at the shining stars with great fascination. 'What if human life exists somewhere up there too?' he wondered. It was impossible to find an answer to this but, who knows, perhaps on one of the stars there was also a Little Buddha lying in a field asking himself the very same question...

When he awoke early in the morning, he had difficulties getting up. His back felt as if it were frozen! The ground had been much too hard and cold – it never got as cold where his Bodhi tree stood, not even in winter. He stretched his whole body and gave himself a good shake, but the pain wouldn't subside. He tried to ignore the unpleasant feeling but that wasn't very successful either. It wasn't until he had walked for a few hours that his back stopped hurting, but only because that pain had been replaced by a new one: instead of an aching back he was now suffering from painful feet, caused by all the walking. And his stomach was rumbling too. He looked around hoping to see a horse carriage that could give him a ride – nothing. In moments like this he didn't enjoy being a traveller at all. But pain and hunger aside, he had to keep walking.

As he advanced towards the mountains with small steps, he thought about the story the gardener had told him. 'Don't hold on, just let go...' So instead of feeling sorry for himself he tried to let his thoughts run freely as well as he could. He accepted the suffering because he couldn't make it disappear, but he could at least stop focusing on it. And indeed, slowly but surely his painful feet and rumbling stomach bothered him less and less. His problems hadn't gone away but next to the pain and the hunger there was now space for other feelings and thoughts, therefore the intensity of the suffering decreased.

*

Just before sunset the Little Buddha reached a well where he could satisfy his thirst. Next to the well a signpost indicated that it was still ten kilometres to the next village – he definitely wouldn't get there before nightfall. Feeling at a loss, he looked around him. Not far from him he saw an old house, maybe he could spend the night there? With renewed courage he walked the short distance to the house and knocked on the old wooden door. Silence. He knocked again, this time a bit harder. Again nothing. When he banged his fists against the door for the third time, it suddenly squeaked and creaked and, before he knew it, the hinges came undone and the door crashed onto the ground in front of him. His petrified heart almost stopped! It took quite a while before he dared to set foot inside and carefully enter the house through the empty doorway. Everything was full of dust and, apart from some spiders, no one seemed to live there. He was standing in a deserted ruin.

Outside it was dark by now and so the Little Buddha decided to spend the night in the run-down building. He dragged the fallen door into one of the rooms, blew away the dust and lay down on the makeshift bed with his blanket. Soon, he fell asleep from exhaustion.

*

The following morning, the Little Buddha was woken by the first rays of sunlight. He got up and wanted to leave right away but then he suddenly heard a long 'crrrr...' He jerked to a halt, but it was already too late.

'Oh, oh...'

He looked down at his robe. It had torn up to his navel and was now in two pieces! The old fabric had got caught on a nail of the broken door and his haste had pulled it apart. The Little Buddha fastened the remaining tatters with a few knots, but it was obvious he wouldn't be able to continue his journey like this. What now? As he stood there wondering what to do, he remembered the signpost he had seen the previous evening. Hadn't it mentioned a nearby village? Surely he would be able to find some new clothes there.

*

After a two-hour walk, the Little Buddha reached the small village. By now he was so hungry his first priority was to find something to eat. Luckily, he soon met the generous owner of a tavern who treated him to a tasty breakfast. The Little Buddha offered to clean the kitchen in exchange for the food but the landlord just shook his head and grinned.

'I'm more than happy to help a young man travelling through.'

The Little Buddha gave him a grateful smile.

'Do you know where I could get a new robe by any chance? My old one just got torn.'

'Yes, there are a few shops in the village.' The man hesitated for a moment. 'But if you want something really special, I recommend you visit the hard-working weaver. She makes the most beautiful, soft and comfortable fabrics you can imagine.'

The Little Buddha loved this suggestion and asked the man for directions to find her.

*

Twenty minutes later he had arrived. The weaver's workshop was on the outskirts of the village and consisted of a big room that was fully open towards the side of the street. High shelves stacked with many different yarns and wool bundles lined the walls, and in the corners lay rolls of already finished fabrics. The first thing the Little Buddha noticed, though, was the incredible range of colours in the room, which gave him a very warm feeling.

The weaver sat at her loom and worked. Combining the different threads required a lot of concentration, and yet she radiated an air of great calmness.

'Hello,' the Little Buddha said.

'Hello,' the weaver replied. 'What can I do for you?'

He pointed to the knotted rags that were dangling from him.

'I need a new robe.'

'Then you've come to the right place! What kind of robe would you like?'

'The same as this one.'

'In orange?'

'Yes, but maybe with some better fabric. I was told that you make particularly soft fabrics.'

'I do my best,' the woman said with a modest smile. 'When do you need it?'

'As soon as possible. I won't be able to wear my old one much longer before it totally rips.'

'Well, you will have to wait a few days. I have quite a bit of work to finish first.' She paused for a moment. 'The day after tomorrow, would that be OK?'

The Little Buddha thought for a moment. He had intended to continue his journey that same day. But of course, he wasn't the weaver's only client and he also understood that she couldn't create beautiful fabric in next to no time. Surely, he'd find a place to stay for a few days.

'Yes, the day after tomorrow is fine. There's one more thing though... I don't have any money.'

'Do you have time?' the weaver asked.

'That I do, plenty of it.'

'Good. How do you feel about helping me for a couple of days? As payment for your robe.'

'That would be perfect,' the Little Buddha answered happily.

The woman stood up from her loom, came towards him and shook his hand.

'Done!'

While the weaver returned to her chair, the Little Buddha began to tidy up the shelves and rearrange all the yarns. Every now and then he turned to the woman and watched her behind her loom. She looked very content with her work.

'Why did you choose this job?' he asked.

'Because clothes and colours have always fascinated me, even as a small child. When I was a bit older, I served an apprenticeship with a master weaver and from day one I was totally hooked.'

'Is it difficult to make a beautiful fabric?'

'Not difficult but you do need to know quite a bit. For example, how the weaving loom works and how to design a new pattern. Sometimes this job can also be quite hard, often I sit here from early in the morning till late at night. I can only take off one day per week, otherwise I wouldn't be able to keep up with all the orders.'

She got up to change one of the reels. Once she had put in new thread, she continued talking without ever taking her eyes off her hands and the slowly growing fabric.

'I really love my trade! It's challenging and sometimes I almost go crazy when I work on a very complicated pattern. But most of the time it gives me great joy to play with the colours and all the different fabrics. And you know what?'

The Little Buddha looked at her in suspense.

'The weaving even creates music! Wooden sounds with a gentle, steady rhythm that help my thoughts flow freely. It's like meditation to me.'

A smile crept over the Little Buddha's face. There are indeed many ways to meditate. In the end what matters is finding a way to give the present moment your full attention.

All day long people arrived with new orders and requests. The man who came in the early evening didn't seem to be very interested in the fabrics though. He brought the woman a big bouquet of flowers and they talked for a while. They laughed a lot and kept looking at each other with gleaming eyes.

'Was that your husband?' the Little Buddha asked when the man had gone.

'No.'

'So why did he give you flowers?'

'Because he would like to be my husband,' she answered briefly.

The next question was already going through his head but before the Little Buddha could say anything the woman changed the subject.

'Where are you going to sleep?'

The Little Buddha shrugged his shoulders.

'If you want you can stay here for the night.'

'Thank you, that's very kind.'

They continued their work in silence. When the last lights were turned off in the village the weaver said good night, took the flowers and went home. The Little Buddha stayed behind by himself. While he made his bed, he wondered about the male visitor – for some reason the woman hadn't wanted to talk about him. But maybe it was simply none of his business. He lay down, tired from the long day, and soon he fell asleep in between all the colourful wool bundles.

*

Just before sunrise the hard-working weaver was already sitting behind her loom again, pulling the threads. The Little Buddha had woken up early too but he treated himself to a cup of tea first before he began his work. He had finished tidying up the shelves, now his job was to coil new yarn onto the empty reels.

It wasn't until midday that they both took a break to eat and rest. Afterwards they continued weaving and coiling and while doing so the time flew by.

*

When the sun was already so low that its rays entered the room, a man with flowers came to visit once again. The Little Buddha was puzzled though because it wasn't the same man from the previous day. Yet just as before, the woman talked to her visitor for a long time and they too looked at each other with gleaming eyes. The Little Buddha had to wait for over half an hour until he was alone with the woman. He was really eager to solve this riddle.

'Does a different man come to bring you flowers every day?'

'No, not every day. And it's just the two.'

'Does the man from today also want to be your husband?'

'Yes, I think so.'

The weaver smiled bashfully.

'But are you allowed to have two husbands?'

'No, of course not.'

The Little Buddha thought about it for a moment.

'And if you were allowed to, would you like to have two?'

'I don't know. I don't think I'd have enough time for two husbands.'

They laughed.

'But seriously, the situation is not that easy. I met them both around the same time and...'

She wasn't sure whether she should tell him the truth. But the Little Buddha already sensed what had happened anyway.

'You've fallen in love with both of them, haven't you?'

'Yes, and they have both fallen in love with me, too. That's why they bring me flowers and other gifts.'

The Little Buddha remembered the woodcutter's wife. Sometimes the things in life were really badly distributed: one got flowers from two different men, the other didn't get any at all.

'You know,' the weaver continued, 'I didn't fall in love with them both on purpose. It just happened.'

'Do you love one of them more than the other?'

'That's what I'm trying to figure out but I haven't been able to decide. And before I forget, please don't tell anybody about this! If others found out there would be a huge drama in the village.'

'Sure, I won't say anything.'

Who would he tell anyway? He was only travelling through.

'What about your two admirers, do they know about one another?'

'Oh no!'

The woman shook her head vigorously.

'And what happens if one day both arrive with flowers at the same time?'

'That would be a disaster! I don't even want to think about that.'

The Little Buddha could well imagine that it would be a rather strange situation but at the same time he didn't understand why the whole issue had to be so complicated.

'Actually, why would it be a drama if others knew about it? After all it's not your fault you've fallen in love with both of them.'

'True, but nobody cares. You can only fall in love with one person, it's always been like this and it will probably always stay like this. And still I wonder, do we really have to restrict love? Isn't it possible that love is big enough to be shared with several people? If I have strong feelings for two men, why does it have to be something bad?'

No, the Little Buddha didn't think it was something bad. Yet he asked himself how the two men would feel about it. Would they be willing to share their wife with another man?

'How would you feel if it was the other way around? If you had fallen in love with a man who loves not only you but also another woman?'

'That's a very good question. I don't know... I've never been in that situation so I can't give you an honest answer to that.'

'And what if you tried to talk to them about your feelings?'

'Yes, I've thought about that as well. But I'm scared they will get angry and that I will end up with no one. I really don't know what to do.'

For a while they quietly dedicated themselves to their work. Later, just before the weaver headed home, the Little Buddha brought up the situation with the two men once more.

'If you want to have a family and children then you have to make a choice at some point. However, if you're not in a hurry and you can't decide right now, then simply wait. Time usually finds a solution for all problems.'

'You're right. Maybe I'm not ready yet to get married. Or maybe neither of the two is the right one for me. Who knows, maybe I'll meet a third one...'

The Hard-working Weaver
67

Chapter 7
The Grateful Mother

ust before noon the hard-working weaver finally finished and handed the Little Buddha his brand-new robe. He took off the old one, put on the new one and was delighted. It was exactly as promised.

'This really is the most beautiful and comfortable fabric I've ever worn!'

He thanked the woman several times and let his hands glide over the wonderful fibres again and again.

Surely, his travels would be even more enjoyable in such an extraordinary piece of clothing!

The time had come to say goodbye. The weaver gave the Little Buddha some bread and fruit for the next leg of his journey. They hoped they would see each other again one day but of course they couldn't know whether this would really happen. Many of the people you meet on your journey through life you will never see again. Often, they are unique encounters and so it's best to enjoy the shared moments as much as possible. Especially if you like someone.

The Little Buddha left the village and walked towards the north in his new robe. The landscape was still flat, but it couldn't be long now until the mountains would appear on the horizon. He was already looking forward to the moment he would see the famous snow-capped peaks for the first time.

*

About an hour after he had set off, he spotted a woman who was heading in the same direction as him. She was walking slowly and carried something on her back, but from a distance he couldn't make out what it was. However, when he caught up with her the mystery of her load was solved at once: she was carrying a baby in a thin scarf. It was only a few months old and was fast asleep.

'Hello,' the Little Buddha whispered.

The woman gave him a friendly smile without saying anything.

'Where are you going?'

'Home.'

'Is it far from here?'

'About two hours.'

'And where have you come from?'

'From the village. I was visiting the doctor because my daughter is ill.'

'Oh, I'm sorry to hear that. What's wrong with her?'

'She has a fever. She hasn't slept for two nights so I started to get really worried. But the doctor said it's nothing serious. He gave me some herbs and told me she will be fine again soon.'

'I'm sure that was a great relief for you.'

'Yes, indeed. In the end it wouldn't have been necessary to take on the long walk to the village but I'm still glad that I did. It could have easily been something more serious. And there is no doctor close to where we live.'

In silence they walked side by side. The Little Buddha wasn't in a hurry and decided to accompany the woman to her house.

'And what about you? Where do you come from and where are you going?' she asked.

'I've spent the last few days with the weaver in the village and before that I spent a few weeks with a friend in his castle garden, a couple of days walk south from here. My home is under a big Bodhi tree and now I'm on the way to the mountains.'

'You get about quite a bit! So what's the reason for your travels?'

'Curiosity! I just love to discover new places and to meet new people. Besides, a while ago someone asked me a question about love. Since I hardly knew anything about love I decided to go on a journey to find out more.'

'And what have you learned so far?'

'That true love is quite difficult to find and that you can't own it once you've found it. And I also know now that you can have butterflies in your stomach. Unfortunately, I haven't had any myself yet, but I hope this will change one day.'

'You want to fall in love?'

'Yes.'

'But are you allowed to do that?'

'Why not?'

'Because you are a Buddha. And Buddhas aren't allowed to have women, are they?'

'Says who?' he asked, astonished and with a hint of indignation. 'I'm just a normal person like everyone else. Why shouldn't I be allowed to fall in love?'

The woman shrugged her shoulders. Then she stopped and turned her face to her child. Her daughter's eyes were still closed and she was breathing peacefully. The mother touched the tiny forehead with great care. Fortunately, the fever had gone down.

*

As they continued walking, the Little Buddha tried to imagine what it would be like to have a child of his own. He had never thought about

having children, up until recently he hadn't even thought about having a romantic relationship.

'Who do you love more, your daughter or your husband?'

'You can't compare the two. I love them both but in very different ways.'

'So how does the love you feel for your child differ from the love you feel for your husband?'

She contemplated his question for a moment.

'I'm afraid the love for my husband is perishable. I hope I will always love him but I can't be sure of it. I will always love my child, though, no matter what happens. And my child also needs me much more than my husband does. For example, today I actually didn't have time to be away all day. We have a small farm and there's always lots of work to do. But the wellbeing of my daughter is much more important than a clean farmhouse or a happy husband. I want her to be healthy and I would do anything for her.'

The woman turned to her baby again.

'She's like a fragile treasure that I need to protect. I would even die for her!'

'Really?'

'Yes. You know, there's nothing worse than seeing your own child suffer. She's a part of me. When she cries, I cry too; when she laughs, I laugh as well.'

'Are you never angry with her?'

'Of course I am. But even then, I love her. And when she cries for nights on end and I'm not able to sleep – it doesn't change the deep feelings I have for her. In such moments it's almost as if I love her without wanting to. It's an unconditional love that I have never felt for any other person.'

She paused.

'It's difficult to understand if you haven't experienced it yourself. It's a very unique feeling that goes way beyond words. Pure love, free of any doubts! To be honest I'm not sure it's actually possible to love a partner unconditionally. Because I expect certain things from my husband – how he treats me, how he treats others, what he says and what he does and especially what he feels. Yet I don't have any expectations of my daughter. And even if I had and they weren't met, I wouldn't love her any less.'

The Little Buddha was almost envious. He had never heard anyone talk about love so beautifully.

'I know I don't own my child,' the woman continued, 'because you can't own a person. But still I feel I was given a precious gift. And for this gift I am eternally grateful.'

*

The landscape was getting steeper but there was still no sign of high mountains. When they had almost reached the farm, darkness set in and so the woman invited the Little Buddha to spend the night in her house. He gladly accepted the offer and was once again amazed by the many kind and generous people he met on his journey.

While they walked the last metres to the house, the woman spoke up again.

'One day, when my daughter is older, she will probably leave me, like almost all children leave their parental home to live independently.

And although I don't want to think about it, sooner or later one of us will die and then our paths will definitely go separate ways. Thanks to the birth of my daughter, I have therefore learned something very valuable.'

It was something the Little Buddha had long known, but it was so important he couldn't be reminded often enough.

'To love life and be grateful for every moment you're here!'

The Grateful Mother

Chapter 8
The Silent Beekeeper

t rained the whole night. Heavy drops poured onto the ground and the air received a thorough spring cleaning. But by the time the Little Buddha resumed his journey early the next morning, the clouds had moved on and the view was blissfully clear. Cheerfully he walked through a long valley, past endless apricot trees in full bloom. In some places it looked as if the whole land had been covered with a rose-coloured carpet. A wonderful sweet scent filled the air and the birds sang happily as he moved along the narrow path at an easy pace.

Soon he reached the end of the valley and had to climb a little hill. When he arrived at the top his breath was taken away, not because the climb had been so hard but because, right in front of him, he saw the massive mountain range the gardener had told him about. The snow-capped peaks were still far away but they already looked much bigger than he had imagined. Like majestic kings they soared into the deep blue sky!

The Little Buddha stood there for a while and stared at the unique panorama before his eyes with great fascination. Then he continued his journey – after all he wanted to meet the mountains at close range.

Without pausing he placed one foot after the other, magically attracted by the miracle of nature rising up in front of him. Just before it got dark, he spotted a small cave by the side of the path. He decided to spend the night there and rest for the day ahead. After a short meditation he fell asleep, exhausted but with a smile on his face.

*

The sun had hardly risen the following morning and the Little Buddha was already on his way again. Slowly he drew closer to the giant peaks, yet they still seemed so far away.

It didn't take long for him to realize that walking through the mountains was literally full of ups and downs. After each steep climb he was rewarded with a breathtaking view and a downhill stroll. But soon the next climb would follow. 'Oh no, another mountain,' he sighed. 'Will it ever stop?' And like this his journey continued, all the way to the top, down to the valley and up again.

The previous day he had been able to walk without interruption but now he had to take regular breaks. It was the hardest part of his journey so far, yet also one of the most beautiful. He drank water from crystal-clear streams, inhaled fresh mountain air and, thanks to the intense movement, he felt as alive as hardly ever before. He saw wild goats, enormous butterflies, and even some eagles gliding peacefully from peak to peak. And the view, that amazing mountain view, was constantly changing – the higher he got, the more impressive it was. If someone had asked him to describe what his eyes saw, he would have been at a loss for words.

*

In the early afternoon he reached a high plain. Next to a big field with blooming flowers there were a few stumps of cork oak trees and on one of them he sat down to rest. He let his eyes wander and allowed his feet a much-deserved break.

When his breath had calmed, he suddenly heard quiet but constant humming. He looked around but he couldn't work out where the unusual sound was coming from. Then he noticed some black dots flying above one of the other tree stumps. He got up and walked towards it to have a closer look, then stopped as if rooted to the spot: the cork oak stump was housing a beehive! Countless little bees buzzed around busily at work. The Little Buddha took a few steps back as a precaution but backed into something. Quickly he turned around to find a strong man with long grey hair standing in front of him.

'I didn't hear you coming,' the Little Buddha said, slightly startled.

The man smiled at him.

'Do you live here in the mountains?' the Little Buddha asked.

The man nodded.

'And what do you do here?'

Without saying a word, the stranger looked at the bees.

'I see, you are the beekeeper.'

The man nodded again. The Little Buddha was confused because he wasn't used to receiving only wordless answers.

'Can't you speak?'

The beekeeper shook his head. Then he pointed his fingers to his ears and nodded.

'You can't speak but you can hear?'

Indeed, the beekeeper was dumb but not deaf. The Little Buddha was able to talk to him by asking questions that could be answered with a nod or a shake of the head.

'Do all your bees live in the same tree stump?'

The beekeeper shook his head and pointed to all the other stumps.

'Are you saying that there are bees even in the stump I was sitting on?'

'Of course,' the beekeeper communicated with a smiling nod.

'But I didn't see any earlier.'

The man pointed to the field.

'Ah, they're collecting nectar.'

Another nod. The field was a sea of flowers, it must have been paradise for the bees. The Little Buddha made a mental note to plant as many flowers as possible as soon as he returned to his Bodhi tree. Because more flowers meant happier bees and the Little Buddha loved to make others happy – whether they were people or bees, it didn't matter to him. After all, every being had a right to be happy.

'How many bees live in each stump?' he asked. 'One hundred?'

The beekeeper knitted his eyebrows and shook his head.

'One thousand?'

Again he shook his head.

'More than a thousand? Ten thousand?'

There were even more than ten thousand in each tree stump. The Little Buddha was seriously impressed and kept silent for a few moments.

'Are bees dangerous?'

The man shrugged his shoulders.

'Does this mean yes or no?'

Another shoulder-shrug. Perhaps he didn't know either? But no, that didn't seem possible considering how much time he spent with the bees.

'Do they never sting you?'

The silent man raised his hand and indicated for the Little Buddha to wait. He approached one of the bee swarms and pulled an angry face. Afterwards he shook his arm as if he had been stung.

'I understand,' the Little Buddha said. 'When you are angry or agitated, they attack you.'

The beekeeper nodded. Then he approached the bee swarm again, this time with a loving smile. He got closer to the tree stump, knelt down carefully reached out his arm. One of the bees landed on his bare skin, then another. Before long his whole arm was covered by the black-and-yellow insects. The Little Buddha watched him with his mouth agape – suddenly he felt speechless too. He had just witnessed what happens when you're not fearful and face life with love and trust instead.

*

After a while the beekeeper gently wiped the bees from his arm. Then he got up and fetched a silver jug from a basket at the side of the path. He took off the lid and blew into it a few times. Shortly after, smoke started to rise out of the jug. He approached the stump once more and carefully blew some smoke into the tiny entrance holes near the bottom. Then he removed a flat piece of wood that covered the empty stump and blew some smoke into the top too. He placed the jug on the ground and reached his hand directly into the hive. The Little Buddha squeezed his eyes shut – he wondered if that really was a good idea. But the beekeeper knew what he was doing. A few seconds later, he retracted his unscathed hand holding a honeycomb dripping with dark, sticky gold. He pushed the piece of wood back over the opening, turned to the Little Buddha and handed him the bees' precious treasure.

'Can I eat it just like that?'

His question was answered with another nod. The Little Buddha dipped his finger into the sticky mass and happily put it into his mouth. He closed his eyes and could hardly believe what was happening on his tongue.

'This is by far the best honey I've ever tasted!'

After he had made sure everything was alright with the other beehives,

the beekeeper directed the Little Buddha to his home. The path led them past a small cedar forest and soon they reached a wooden hut where the beekeeper lived with his wife.

*

Back at the hut, the beekeeper went into a back room to tidy up his work equipment while his wife greeted the Little Buddha. Full of enthusiasm, he told her about his encounter with the bees. The moment the beekeeper's arm had been entirely covered by the buzzing insects had touched him especially deeply.

'Even though they all have a poisonous sting, they were totally peaceful,' he recounted.

'Well, they are very peaceful beings by nature,' the woman said. 'You know, bees are very sensitive – they sense if someone is scared or wants to hurt them, or if someone has come with good intentions. They might not be able to understand what people say but they can perceive feelings and react to them.'

She paused for a moment.

'Us humans can pick up on the feelings of others too, even if it happens unconsciously. If we listen to our inner voice, we don't need words to know whether someone likes us or not, whether someone tells the truth or lies, whether someone loves or hates.'

Again there was silence.

'Would you like some tea?' the woman asked.

'Yes please.'

She disappeared into the kitchen to boil water. At the same moment the silent beekeeper entered the room and handed the Little Buddha a piece of paper that was filled with beautiful handwriting on both sides.

'What is it?' the Little Buddha asked. 'A story?'

Yes, it was a story.

'Did you write it?'

The beekeeper nodded in his warm, calm manner, as if he wanted to say that it wasn't important who had written it. And so the Little Buddha began to read.

*

A long time ago a queen and her daughter lived in a faraway land. The daughter was very beautiful and had many admirers. When she was old enough to marry, she was supposed to choose her future husband. The princess picked three admirers, but she couldn't decide which of the three would make the best husband. So she asked her mother for help. The queen ordered the three men to appear before the royal court and gave them a task: 'Go to the forest and bring my daughter fresh honey!'

The next morning, the admirers set off. The first one found a small beehive on that same day. Slowly he moved closer, step by step. But then a bee stung him right on his nose. Frightened, he turned around and ran as if his life were in danger. He arrived at the palace empty-handed and delivered the disappointing news to the princess.

The second man had also seen a small beehive but, ambitious as he was, he wanted to bring the princess a whole barrel of honey. So, he continued his search and after a few days he found a gigantic beehive. Courageously he walked towards it, but he too got stung in the face. Instead of getting scared, though, like the first man, he got very angry and started to strike out in all directions. His frantic movements aroused the whole bee population and while he tried to collect the precious honey more and more bees attacked him, in defence of their home. When he was covered with stings from head to toe, he finally gave up and returned to the princess without honey. He was actually very lucky he had made it out alive.

The third admirer also found a beehive, one that was neither big nor small. Carefully he approached it, but, just like the others, he got stung too. Yet instead of running away in a panic or attacking the bees, he simply moved back a few metres, sat down on a fallen tree trunk and waited. He watched the small insects busily living their lives and thought about how he could gain their trust. Finally, he had an idea: he went to a nearby stream, filled an old piece of bark with water and placed it next to the beehive. Soon the bees went to the bark to quench their thirst. The man stayed close by for several days. He brought them fresh water and waited patiently, hoping that soon they would no longer see him as a threat. And indeed, after one week he cautiously approached them and none of the bees stung him. They simply kept working and even allowed him to take some of their sweet food. The man gave his thanks to the bees and returned to the palace with a jar full of honey.

The marriage took place just one week later and, from then on, the princess and her husband lived happily ever after.

A few years later the princess asked her mother how she had known that the challenge of finding honey would help her choose the right man.

'Love is like a beehive,' the queen said. 'It can hurt you, even kill you – but it can also give you the sweetest honey you've ever tasted. If you want the honey you mustn't be greedy and steal everything from the bees. You have to treat them well and you always have to respect them. And you shouldn't be afraid to get hurt. Otherwise you will run away after the first sting.'

The Silent Beekeeper

Chapter 9
The Magic Lake

nce again, the Little Buddha had been lucky to be in the right place, at the right time. Through the encounter with the silent beekeeper he had not only met the bees but had also found a place to spend his time in the mountains.

The beekeeper and his wife were delighted to have a visitor because they rarely had a chance to welcome people into their home. Even their closest friends hardly ever came to visit – most villages were too far away and the steep climb to their hut was too exhausting. So they seized the opportunity and treated their special guest to fresh teas from the herb garden and thickly coated honey breads, of which the Little Buddha couldn't get enough.

*

During the daytime the beekeeper took him to the fields on the high plateau and showed him how he worked with the bees. The Little Buddha observed everything with great fascination. He was seriously considering putting up some beehives himself once he returned to his Bodhi tree. The only problem was that, as a Buddha, he had to try not to develop any major desires for anything, because desires always increase suffering. If you don't get what you want, you end up dissatisfied, and if you do get it you start to worry you might lose it again. But the honey was simply too tasty – perhaps he could make a little exception...

In the evenings the three of them spent many cosy hours in front of the open fire. The beekeeper's wife often shared stories about life in the mountains and talked about the daily challenges, the hard work, the loneliness and the long winters. At the same time, she loved the heavenly peace up there, she spoke of unlimited freedom and of the wonderful wild nature that mesmerized her every day.

*

The Little Buddha enjoyed the pleasant company to the fullest. After a few weeks, however, he felt like spending some time alone again. One evening he turned to his hosts and asked them if they knew a nice route for a day trip. The woman smiled mysteriously and gave him directions that, according to her, would lead him to a truly extraordinary place. She didn't want to tell him what exactly awaited him there but the word 'extraordinary' had been enough to make the Little Buddha curious. The next morning he got up early, packed some food into his bag and set off shortly after sunrise.

*

The Little Buddha set off through the forest at a placid pace at first, but soon the relaxed stroll was over. The path got more and more rugged and steep and there was no end in sight! He was wheezing and struggling upwards metre by metre. Again and again he had to pause and wipe the sweat from his eyes. He wondered whether the woman had actually sent him up one of the gigantic peaks. Surely the view would be amazing up there but how was he supposed to make it? After all he wasn't a mountain climber but just a normal hiker.

By now he had passed the treeline, and the path was surrounded by thick scrub and rough cliffs. He was just about to give up and walk back when suddenly the gradient flattened. And then, out of nowhere, his destination appeared in front of him: an enormous mountain lake!

'How beautiful!' he shouted, feeling exhilarated. The overwhelming sight made him forget the struggles of the ascent at once.

The lake shimmered shiny and blue and the surface was so smooth the peaks and the white clouds were mirrored perfectly. For several minutes the Little Buddha didn't move and just admired with great humbleness the unique piece of art nature had created in this remote place. It was like so often in life: the best treasures are well hidden and can only be discovered when you're prepared to leave your comfort zone.

The sweat was still running down his forehead and his back after the exhausting climb. It was a beautiful day in late spring, the sun was shining and there was almost no wind – perfect conditions to have a refreshing bath. He was about to take off his robe but decided to be on the safe side by dipping his big toe into the water first. He jerked it back immediately – the lake was freezing cold! 'What a shame,' he thought, 'it looked so inviting'. But his heart would probably have stopped if he had dived into it. So instead of going for a swim he just splashed some water on his face and sat down on a flat stone close to the water's edge.

*

After absorbing the impressive landscape for a while, the Little Buddha closed his eyes and began to meditate. He focused on his breath and observed how the fresh air flowed in and out of his nose slowly and steadily. Like always, he managed to keep this up quite well for a few moments but then an army of random thoughts started to invade his peaceful mind.

First the wonderful images of the mountains tried to distract him. Then his stomach rumbled, and he had to think about the delicious honey bread in his bag, waiting to be eaten. He registered the thought and returned to his breath. Yet soon the mental whirlwind continued: the conversation from the previous day, what was it the woman had said? And the way back to the hut, would he make it safely down the hill? Then he suddenly thought about love, about everything he had learned so far. Back to the breath. Stillness. Then again the honey bread that was so terribly tasty. And he was thirsty too. Then love again – what if he never fell in love? He so wanted to experience what it felt like to have butterflies flying through his stomach. Images rushed into his head: the bees in the beehive, his Bodhi tree, the blue lake. Stop! Inhaling, exhaling. In and out, in and out. Then his right foot complained because it had fallen asleep. Back to the honey bread, love, the mountains, thirst – and so it went on and on.

The Little Buddha had been practising meditation for many years and knew thoughts couldn't simply be switched off. His mind was a passionate wanderer, just like himself. The only thing he could do was not hold on to the thoughts but let them roam freely and keep bringing the focus back to his breath. Because, unlike thoughts, the breath is never in the past or future. It's a safe harbour in the present and that's exactly what matters: always returning to the here and now!

Gradually the thoughts lost their power and it became easier for the Little Buddha to observe his inhalations and exhalations. Then suddenly everything went quiet, both in his head and around him. A feeling of profound peace spread through him, a silent blissfulness he had experienced only a few times before. It was as if the snow-capped peaks were laying a protective hand over this special moment, keeping kind of noise and distraction away from him.

The Little Buddha had no idea how long this moment lasted but to him it seemed like a small eternity. It was only when he heard the distant sound of a mountain goat that he slowly opened his eyes again. As if in a trance, he stared at the smooth lake and felt deep contentment. How lucky he was to experience so many unique moments!

*

After an extensive picnic, the Little Buddha decided to walk around the lake. Halfway around, he reached a rock that protruded a few metres above the water. He ventured to the edge, cautiously sat down and let his legs dangle in the air.

Once again he thought about all the love stories he had heard so far. Why were people so obsessed with finding someone they could love? Their whole happiness seemed to depend on it. Wasn't it possible to be happy without a partner? After all, everyone is born alone and dies alone. Surely it must be wonderful to share your life with someone you like, but does it make sense to be sad just because you're alone? Isn't it much better to know you can be happy even without another person? He rose up and looked down onto the crystal clear water, lost in thought. And then, while observing his reflection on the surface of the lake, he suddenly realized where love truly came from – from deep within!

The only person he would always be together with was himself. Therefore, it was most important to love exactly that person first and foremost. Because how can you love someone else if you don't love yourself?

The Little Buddha raised his head and let his eyes wander. A dry lake wouldn't be able to share a single drop of water, not with the animals or the people, nor the rivers or the clouds. Even worse, without water every lake would be dead.

And without self-love no one is happy.

*

He spent the whole day at the lakeside and lost track of the time. It wasn't until it started to get dark that he remembered he still had a long way back to the beekeeper's hut. In haste he picked up his bag and was just about to set off when he noticed something white glistening on the water's surface. He looked up and saw the full moon rising between the snow-capped peaks. His heart began to glow, and he felt infinite gratitude. A small tear rolled down his cheek.

It was truly an extraordinary place. A magic lake, hidden amongst majestic mountains.

Chapter 10
The Healing Hands

It had already been dark for quite some time when the Little Buddha finally reached the hut. The beekeeper and his wife had been worried because the mountains can easily turn into a dangerous labyrinth at night – especially for someone who is not familiar with the surroundings. Greatly relieved, they greeted their guest when he entered the hut with a happy smile.

The Little Buddha joined them in front of the fireplace and shared all the details of his incredible day trip to the magic lake. He told them about how he had observed his own reflection and how he had realized that you can't love anyone without loving yourself. His hosts nodded in agreement, they had already been to the lake many times themselves and had lived very similar experiences. To them it seemed as if every drop of the lake was filled with endless wisdom.

*

For a while all three sat in silence. The only movement in the room was the gentle flickering of the fire. Then the beekeeper tried to get the Little Buddha's attention. He obviously wanted to tell him something in sign language. He folded his arms in front of his chest, raised his right hand and extended both arms to the front. The Little Buddha made a real effort to understand him but he couldn't figure out what he was trying to sign. He looked to the woman for help.

'He says that love means giving someone your time,' she translated. 'Because time is the most precious thing we can share with another person.'

'So, self-love means to give time to myself,' the Little Buddha concluded.

'Yes. Because you need time to get to know yourself and find out what your strengths and weaknesses are. And only once you know who you really are can you learn to fully accept yourself. Without acceptance there is no love – not for yourself nor for anyone else.'

She paused for a moment.

'And it's also important to treat yourself to something nice every now and then. Like you did today, for example, spending a day alone in nature. Or to meditate, to make yourself a nice meal or to get a massage.'

The Little Buddha started to daydream.

'A massage... that must be wonderful!'

'Are you trying to tell me you've never received a massage?'

With a sad expression in his eyes the Little Buddha shook his head.

'Who would have massaged me? My friend the farmer? No, he has other things to do.'

The woman gave him a compassionate look.

'I can't imagine a life without massages. My husband and I often massage each other. As he cannot speak, we've learned to communicate in different ways. And believe me, speaking with your hands is much more powerful than words could ever be. There are things that simply cannot be described with words. Especially when it comes to love – you have to feel it and the best way to do that is to let your body do the talking!'

There was silence again.

'You know what?' the woman suddenly said. 'I just remembered my sister is coming to visit us tomorrow. She's a true artist with her hands! Maybe she can give you a massage too.'

'Really? Do you think she would do that?'

'Sure, why not?'

'Doesn't she have a husband?'

'No. And even if she did, a massage doesn't mean you have to get married straight away!'

That's true, the Little Buddha thought.

'When she gets here tomorrow, I will ask her if she can give you your first ever massage.'

His face lit up in anticipation.

'That would be great!'

*

The next day, shortly after noon, the sister of the beekeeper's wife arrived at the hut. She came to fetch new honey every three weeks, which she then sold in a small shop in the village. The beekeeper's wife took her sister aside and told her about the conversation from the previous evening. With a smile she agreed to massage the Little Buddha, even though she didn't have much time because she had to return to her village that same day.

*

When the Little Buddha entered the back room of the hut, he could hardly believe his eyes. He had expected a dark chamber but what he encountered was the exact opposite: a spacious room with a big window that allowed the warm afternoon sun to enter. Incense sticks diffused a pleasant scent. On the wall next to him there was a beautiful painting of a lotus flower. The sister of the beekeeper's wife stood by the window and greeted him by bowing her head. Then she pointed to a couple of

sheepskins on the wooden floor.

'Shall I lie down there?'

'If you want you can also stand,' the woman grinned, 'but a massage is much more fun when you're lying down.'

The Little Buddha smiled timidly. He was excited to receive his first massage but he was also a bit nervous because he didn't know what was awaiting him.

'Please take off your robe.'

'Really?'

'Yes. Don't worry, if you get cold, I have a warm blanket.'

The cold was the last thing on the Little Buddha's mind. He had never felt the touch of a woman on his bare skin, least of all on his entire body. For a moment he hesitated but then he took off his robe and lay face downwards on the sheepskins. He had no reason to distrust the woman, surely everything was going to be alright.

'First with your face upwards please.'

'Fine,' he thought, glad he had been allowed to keep at least his waistcloth on.

The woman noticed that the Little Buddha was still uneasy and so she began the massage by carefully grasping his feet with her warm hands.

'You know, it's really important for people to touch each other,' she said with a calm and pleasant voice. 'It doesn't matter how you do it, you can give someone a hug, a massage or simply hold hands.'

'I hug my friends occasionally but I'm alone most of the time.'

'You should hug them more often then, whenever you're with them.'

She began to gently massage his feet.

'Admittedly it's easier for women. Most men have a problem with touching each other. Unless they're married, they hardly ever have physical contact with other human beings. It can make you feel very lonely, don't you think?'

The Little Buddha had never thought about it. But the woman was right, when he exchanged a heartfelt hug with a friend it was impossible to feel lonely.

'So why is it easier for women to touch each other?' he wanted to know.

'That's a good question. Perhaps it's because men think too much, hence their lives take place mainly in their heads whereas women have a stronger need for sensuality. But there are many exceptions, it's not the same for every man and every woman.'

She slowly let her hands glide over his calves, all the way to the knees and then down the other side, back to the feet. After a while she changed her position. When she touched his thighs, the Little Buddha flinched.

'Don't think, feel! Get out of your head, you won't need it now.'

While she started to massage his muscles, the Little Buddha tried to focus his attention on his body.

'What do you feel?'

He took a few deep breaths and observed the sensations in his legs. Little by little he began to relax and enjoy the unusual physical contact. The warm hands of the woman kneaded his thighs like dough and the longer she did this the softer his muscles seemed to become.

'It feels fantastic, please continue!'

The woman smiled but the Little Buddha couldn't see this anymore because he had already closed his eyes and dived deeper and deeper into his body.

After a while she changed over to his hands and massaged each finger, the palms and wrists. Then the forearms, the elbows, the upper arms and finally his belly and chest.

'Okay, now please turn around.'

The Little Buddha slowly rolled on to his side before getting comfortable on his belly. While he was lying there, almost in a trance, he heard the woman open a bottle.

'Just to let you know, this might be a bit cold for a moment.'

Before he could ask what she was about to do, he already felt something dripping onto his bare back.

'What is it?'

'It's a very special oil that is really good for massages.'

'Oil? What kind of oil?'

'Black sesame oil mixed with sandalwood. It will help you to relax even more.'

The woman began to spread the oil across his back with gentle movements. She let her smooth hands glide between his shoulders and over his back, up and down and from side to side. The lovely smelling oil quickly heated up and soon the Little Buddha felt as if warm waves were stroking his skin. When the woman started to hum a peaceful melody, he finally surrendered completely. His last thoughts dissolved, and he let himself fall into the realm of the senses. He felt all the cells in his body floating around and melting into each other, how they danced to the rhythm of these healing hands, lost in pure bliss. And then suddenly time ceased to exist and the Little Buddha became one with the moment.

*

When he came round again, he found the woman sitting next to him with her eyes half-closed. He stared at her, unable to put into words what had just happened. It wasn't actually necessary for him to say anything because the woman knew exactly how he felt. It took several minutes before he broke the silence.

'Wow!'

He shook his head in disbelief and slowly got up.

'I would have never imagined that a massage could be so magical. Where did you learn to use your hands in this way?'

'With an old master, many years ago she taught me her healing art. Although it's really not that difficult, you just need some practice – and lots of loving affection!'

She gave the Little Buddha a glass of water. He was still overwhelmed by the experience.

'It felt as if I was connected to everything!'

'You are,' the woman said, slowly getting ready to leave. 'We are all connected to everything, always. Most of the time we're simply not aware of it. We think that we are totally separate beings who walk through life all alone but in reality, we're not alone at all.'

'Maybe that's what true love means,' the Little Buddha thought out loud. 'To be one with all people, all animals and plants and stones and with everything that exists.'

The woman smiled at him, happy to see the Little Buddha had understood what she had wanted to tell him: that the feeling of separation is one of life's greatest illusions.

The Healing Hands

Chapter 11
The Lonely Monk

e stayed with the silent beekeeper and his wife for a few more days, then the Little Buddha felt it was time to move on and continue his journey.

'Where do you want to go next?'

'I think I will slowly head back towards my Bodhi tree.'

'Do you miss home?' the woman asked.

'Yes, sometimes, but it's not a problem. It's just that I've already been away a couple of months, that's enough for me for now.'

'I hope you know you can stay with us for as long as you want.'

'That's very kind, thank you!'

For a moment the Little Buddha considered extending his stay in the mountains. But then he shook his head.

'I've already met so many new people and had so many new experiences, I really need to let it all sink in. Besides, my journey isn't over yet – who knows what I will experience on my way home.'

The following morning, he packed his blanket and some provisions into his bag and said goodbye to his wonderful hosts.

'I'm glad I met you and that we got to spend some time together. Come and visit me one day as well, you're always most welcome.'

The silent beekeeper and his wife smiled.

'We don't usually go anywhere, but you never know...'

They hugged each other and hoped that someday, somewhere they'd meet again. Then the Little Buddha turned around and was back on the road again.

*

It was a marvellous spring day with bright blue skies and pleasant temperatures. Whistling a happy tune, he marched towards the west, with the mountains to his right and the next, still unknown, chapter of his journey ahead of him.

At first the narrow path led him over some steep hills, making him sweat. But soon the worst was over, and he no longer had to struggle. He was walking mostly downhill now, past colourful fields of flowers, through shady forests and over small streams that carried fresh water into the valley.

After a longer rest in the late afternoon the Little Buddha had just set off again when he noticed dark clouds gathering around the peaks. He immediately remembered the words of the beekeeper's wife who had warned him that the weather in the mountains is prone to rapid changes. The sky above him was still bright blue, though, and there was no wind either – he didn't think the clouds could catch up with him. Without concern and full of confidence he kept walking.

*

About an hour later he took another break and thought about where he might be able to spend the night. The easiest thing would be to sleep under a tree, like he often did. There was still some time until nightfall, though. Before moving on, he bent over the stream in front of him and washed his face. He closed his eyes and relished the cooling water slowly running over his skin. Then all of sudden a loud thunderclap ended his peaceful moment. Startled, he turned around. The mountains had already disappeared behind a black wall of dark clouds that were quickly coming closer. The thunder roared once more and lightning struck only a few metres from him. The Little Buddha jumped to his feet, grabbed his bag and started to run. Maybe he could escape the storm if he was fast enough. But his desperate attempt was in vain: less than five minutes later he was hit by the first raindrops. The wind grew stronger and colder with each moment and he could hear the sound of torrential rain hitting the ground behind him. He didn't even dare to look back, and continued to run along the path as quickly as he could.

*

Spending the night under a tree was no longer a good idea – he'd get soaked, he'd be cold and he could even be struck by lightning. He began to worry. Where would he find shelter?

He stopped for a moment, took a deep breath and looked around. There! In between some trees he saw something white shimmering through. Maybe he could sit the storm out over there. He rushed over to find a small building. Lucky him!

The house was made of flat stones and, on the top of the dark-red roof, colourful prayer flags blew wildly in the wind. It had to be a monastery. The Little Buddha was about to knock when he saw the door was already ajar. In that same moment it began to rain heavily so he decided to enter without knocking.

A big, dark, seemingly empty room opened up in front of him. It wasn't until his eyes adjusted to the low light that he noticed a small altar in the far corner. A lonely candle was burning on top of it. Next to the altar a monk sat wrapped-up in a woollen blanket, with only his bald head peeking out. The Little Buddha approached him cautiously and bowed politely.

'I'm very sorry for invading your space like this,' he said, 'but the storm has caught me by surprise.'

'Don't worry, you're welcome to spend the night here if you want.'

'Thank you!' the Little Buddha replied, greatly relieved. He unpacked his blanket, wrapped it around himself and sat down on a cushion that was lying on the floor. In the meantime, the monk reached for the teapot next to him and poured his visitor a small cup.

'Here, but be careful, it's still very hot.'

For a while they sat in silence and listened to the rain rattling onto the roof.

'Do you live here?'

'Yes.'

'Alone?'

The monk nodded. He gave the Little Buddha a friendly look but there were also traces of deep sadness in his face. Especially in his eyes.

'So why do you live here all by yourself?' the Little Buddha asked, curious as he was.

'That's a long story.'

'Would you like to tell me?'

The monk hesitated. He didn't normally like to talk about his private life, least of all with strangers. But although they had met only a few minutes ago he felt the Little Buddha was different from most other people he knew. For some reason he trusted him.

'Fine. But be warned, it's not a nice story.'

So while the storm raged outside he told the Little Buddha why he lived in the monastery all on his own.

*

'When I was a young man, I met a beautiful woman. It was love at first sight for both of us – we knew instantly that we belonged together. Soon we got married, moved into a house and spent several years in total bliss. Then I noticed something was wrong. My wife had started to distance herself from me more and more, and finally the day arrived when she confessed she didn't love me any more. And to make matters even worse, she told me she had fallen in love with another man.

'I didn't understand what was happening to me and could no longer make sense of the world. How was it possible her love for me had ceased to exist? I still loved her as much as I did on our first day together, even more than that! I simply wouldn't and couldn't accept it. For weeks after our separation I was very angry because I felt betrayed. But soon the anger gave way to endless grief and I fell into a deep, black hole – to me it felt as if my wife had died. Nothing felt right any more and my poor heart was in so much pain I could hardly bear it. I tried to drown my sorrow in alcohol, but it only made everything worse. I even thought about ending my life a few times but I lacked the courage, and then doubts emerged. What if she suddenly decided to return to me and everything could go back to how it was before? For many months this tiny shimmer of hope kept me alive.

'But as much as I wished for it, nothing changed. I became sadder and sadder, and life in the village turned into agony. Every time I saw a happy couple walk by, my broken heart screamed in pain. In the end, I couldn't bear it any longer and decided to withdraw from the mundane world: I joined a monastery and became a monk. I thought perhaps God could heal my wounds. But God didn't manage to reduce my suffering either. I saw how content the other monks were, and this made me feel even worse. I had to leave and go as far away as possible, to a place where I could be alone with my grief. So I roamed the land until I found this deserted monastery. That was almost five

years ago now, and since then I've lived in solitude, hidden away from any civilization.'

*

Silence.

'No, that's not a nice story,' the Little Buddha concluded sadly. 'Do you feel better in solitude at least?'

'No, not really. But I don't know what else to do. I still miss my wife but of course I can't force her to love me. The only good thing up here in the mountains is that I'm not constantly reminded of how beautiful it is to be loved and to be happy.'

'I can imagine it was difficult to lose the woman you loved so much. But maybe you don't really miss the person – maybe you simply miss the feeling she gave you.'

The monk thought about it for a moment.

'That's possible but how does it change my situation?'

'Well, obviously you can't replace your wife but somewhere there might be another woman who can give you love.'

'Yes, maybe... But even if that were the case, unfortunately my experience has shown me that in the end love will lead to suffering anyway.'

'Does that mean you never want to fall in love again?'

Once more the monk was silent.

'I just don't think that I will meet someone else as special as her. And I'm not sure I could actually fall in love again. You know, all the grieving and shedding of tears has formed an invisible scab around my heart. Like a knight's armour it protects me from further pain but at the same time it doesn't let any nice feelings in either.'

A loud thunderclap caused the roof of the monastery to tremble. It was still raining relentlessly, the storm was raging over their heads.

'What about taking off the armour?'

'I don't know... My heart longs for love and affection but it also feels very fragile. I'm afraid to get hurt again, to be badly disappointed once more.'

The Little Buddha noticed how the gloom of the man slowly spilled over to him. Suddenly he felt sorry for all the people who wanted to be in love but weren't. He felt their pain, their yearning and their terrible loneliness. Surely there's no one in the world who doesn't have a deep desire for connection. Even those who doubt love are looking for it – and they need it more than anyone else. Because life without love, well, what kind of life is that? No light and no warmth, always darkness and icy coldness.

*

While the monk poured more tea into their cups, the Little Buddha thought about how he could encourage him to take off the heavy armour. Which words would help to reduce his overwhelming fear and break through his miserable loneliness? The situation was anything but easy and the Little Buddha didn't have a magic remedy for every problem either. But he wanted to at least try. There had to be something he could say to give new life to the dried-up hope of the man.

Finally, he had an idea.

'Do you like flowers?'

The monk looked surprised by the question and nodded.

'Sure, everyone likes flowers.'

'And have you ever seen a withered flower?'

'Of course. Why do you ask?' the monk wondered, slightly irritated.

'To show you that it's natural that a flower doesn't bloom forever. No matter how pretty it is, at some point it loses its petals and dies. As long as it blooms it gives you a lot of joy, but then one day it stops blooming and has nothing left to give. The flower doesn't have any bad intentions, it's just the way it is. Perhaps you're sad because it was a very special flower but at the same time you could also be grateful for the beautiful moments the flower shared with you. And luckily there are seeds! They grow and become small plants which then begin to carry buds and soon turn into new flowers.'

Slowly but surely the monk understood what the Little Buddha was trying to tell him.

'And you think it's the same with love?'

'No, not the same, but similar. Just because one flower withers, it doesn't mean that others won't blossom. Of course, every flower is unique, you can't expect to find the same one twice. But there are millions of flowers – it would be absurd to think there isn't another one you can fall in love with. It might take some time to find the right one but if you're patient and don't give up there's no reason why it shouldn't happen. However, you first have to put the withered flower aside and walk through life with empty hands.'

'And what if I find another favourite flower and one day it leaves me as well? We've just talked about that: the suffering would start all over again.'

'Yes, that's true, but I'm afraid you can't change that. Life, and I think that includes love too, is impermanent. If you don't accept this, you will have to experience a lot of pain indeed.'

They listened to the storm lashing wildly around the house. The Little Buddha felt bad for having said those last words because he knew the monk would have preferred to hear something else. But it was the truth – should he have lied to him?

'Impermanence has a good side, though,' he eventually continued, 'because pain and grief and all the bad times won't last forever either.'

'I know,' the monk said, 'but nevertheless my heart still aches.'

The Little Buddha gave him a compassionate look.

'Maybe you first have to forgive your ex-wife fully before you can let her go. And perhaps you also have to forgive yourself for all the pain you've held on to for so long.'

He paused for a moment.

'If you free your heart from the burden of the past it can open up to new love again.'

'And how am I supposed to do that?'

'You don't have to do anything. You just have to understand that everything which was doesn't exist anymore. The past is a story, nothing more. It only lives in your thoughts.'

'So, I should stop thinking?'

'No. But try to think about something else more often. About the here and now!'

They talked late into the night, accompanied by the drumming of the raindrops. Eventually their eyes began to close. Just before he fell asleep, the Little Buddha turned to the monk once more.

'Whether we like it or not, pain and grief are part of life. But one thing you must always remember: no matter how big it is, behind every cloud there's always blue sky.'

Chapter 12
The Generous Chef

he next morning the clouds had passed on. It was a peaceful spring day and it was strange to think that, only a few hours earlier, a violent storm had raged through the place. Sometimes the weather can change really quickly – just like everything else in life.

The Little Buddha wished the lonely monk all the best and continued his journey. By now the path led downhill all the way, allowing the Little Buddha to advance easily. The sun warmed his skin and all around him nature blossomed in all its glory – it wouldn't be long until summer arrived and the dark winter would be nothing more than a distant memory.

While he strolled along, the Little Buddha thought about his home which was only a few days' walk away. On one hand he felt as though he hadn't seen his Bodhi tree for half an eternity; on the other hand, he felt as if he had only set off yesterday. A mixture of melancholy and anticipation arose inside of him. It was a shame his journey had almost come to an end but at the same time he could hardly wait to finally return home.

*

In the late afternoon he arrived in the lowlands and took a longer break. He meditated for a while and even indulged in a short nap because, despite looking forward to getting home, he wasn't in a hurry. Once he had rested enough, he set off again. He had already been walking for a few minutes when he suddenly remembered that he had forgotten something important. He stopped, turned around and said goodbye to his new friends, the mountains, with a grateful smile on his face.

After spending the night in a deserted barn, he passed a small house around midday the following day. On the covered terrace he saw a table and two benches and next to the entrance door a big pot hung over a blazing fire. A delicious smell rose from the pot, reminding the Little Buddha that he hadn't eaten anything since the previous day. Just as his stomach began to rumble, an old woman came out of the house and greeted him with a friendly smile.

'What a great day, isn't it?'

Using a long wooden spoon, she stirred the pot.

'You will have to wait a little bit, the food isn't ready yet. But you're welcome to take a seat. Would you like a glass of water?'

The Little Buddha looked surprised – he hadn't even asked her whether he could have some food and some water. But without having to be told twice he sat down on one of the benches.

'That's very kind of you,' he said, 'I just hope I'm not disturbing anything.'

'What should you be disturbing?' the woman asked, slightly confused by the question.

'Well, it looks like you're waiting for guests.'

'I am. And you're one of them!'

'But you didn't know I was coming.'

'No, of course not. I never know exactly who is coming but the seats never stay empty.'

'Are you running a restaurant?' the Little Buddha asked carefully. 'Because if you are, I have to tell you I don't have any money.'

The woman laughed heartily.

'Don't worry, I don't want any money for my food. It's enough for me when my guests enjoy it.'

'And what kind of guests do you usually have?'

'Travellers, workers, beggars – anyone who's hungry. I cook for them every day to make sure they get a warm meal.'

She stirred the big pot again.

'And why do you do that?'

'Because I love to cook. And I also love to share because sharing makes me happy.'

The Little Buddha looked at her admiringly. How wonderful to know people like this existed. But he still didn't really understand why she wouldn't charge anything for her work.

'And you never take any money for your food?'

She shook her head.

'How is that possible? Are you rich?'

'No, but my husband and I have a small farm and there's enough food growing in the fields to share with others as well. Besides, you don't have to be rich to be able to share. Everyone can give whatever he or she has, no matter whether it's a lot or just a tiny bit. And you know what?'

The Little Buddha looked at her with waiting eyes.

'Only those who share are truly rich. Not rich with money but rich with love.'

They smiled at each other and fell silent for a moment.

'Do you know the story about the two flute players?' she asked.

'No.'

'It's one of my favourite stories, it really happened like this. Wait, I have to put more wood on the fire.'

The woman disappeared behind the house and returned soon after

with some logs which she carefully placed onto the embers underneath the pot. Then she sat down next to the Little Buddha and told him the story.

*

Many years ago, there were two brothers who were passionate and very talented flute players. They lived on the outskirts of a big town and played their instruments every day. The older of the two practised a lot, often late into the night, because he wanted to become the best flute player in the whole country. He played the scales up and down countless times and learned the most complex pieces. Only rarely did he leave the house.

One day the younger brother decided to go into town and play on the street. He wanted to share the wonderful sounds with others. His older brother turned his nose up at him.

'Simple people don't appreciate our music. I'm telling you, you're wasting your time. You're better off staying at home to practise.'

But the younger brother went ahead with his plan anyway and began to play his flute in the central marketplace every afternoon. The people were very happy to hear the music and soon the number of his listeners grew. After a few weeks he was joined by a drummer, and not long after that, by a sitar player and a singer. Full of joy and enthusiasm they made music together and enriched the everyday life of the town people with their art.

In the meantime, the older brother continued to spend every day alone in his room and practised like a madman, driven by the desire to be the best and to become famous.

A few months went by like this. Then, one evening, the younger brother came running into the house.

'The mayor visited us today and has invited us to play at the big fair

next week!'

The older brother looked at him incredulously.

'Are you serious?'

'Of course. You'll come too, won't you?'

Up until then, the older brother hadn't gone to any of the daily performances. He still thought it was a complete waste of time to play on the street.

'Maybe,' he said indifferently, trying to hide his envy.

The day of the big performance arrived. Although it had cost him quite a bit of effort, the older brother also mingled among the crowd. He witnessed a fantastic concert – every song caused his skin to erupt in goosebumps and he saw smiling faces all around. At the end of the show the people were so excited they wouldn't stop clapping.

As the group played a final encore, the older brother suddenly realized how stupid he had been. Having always practised alone in his chamber might have made him a better flute player but it hadn't touched him or anyone else. He realized that music was like love: it had to be shared! Because only through sharing can it grow.

That same evening, he asked his brother and the other musicians if he could join them. They agreed at once, and from then onwards he was a part of the group and helped to carry the wonderful sounds into the world.

*

When the woman had finished the story, she got up and tended to the food again.

'Love needs exchange,' she continued while adding some spices to the pot. 'It only works by giving-and-taking – it only blossoms when it's shared.'

'And what if you don't have anyone to share with?' the Little Buddha wondered.

The woman looked at him puzzled.

'Well, unless you live on a lonely island that's impossible. There is always someone you can share with: family, friends, neighbours and colleagues, and of course all the strangers you meet and who only remain strangers until you approach them with an open heart.'

'But surely there are also people who have nothing to share. Not everyone has a garden and not everyone can cook like you.'

'That's true but you can also give something of yourself, something very personal. A smile, for example. Believe me, sometimes a smile can be more valuable than material things. And the most precious thing you can share is your own time.'

*

While they continued talking, the other guests arrived. The first one was a merchant who was travelling through; a little later, two beggars from the nearby village turned up. The group was completed by a young woman and her child, both friends of the host. They all sat down at the table and the chef served them a delicious meal of vegetable soup, rice and freshly baked bread. Each guest praised her for her outstanding cooking skills. After the meal, everyone stayed for some tea and the merchant entertained them with funny stories from his travels. It was a relaxed atmosphere and everybody got on well, it was almost like a small family gathering. When the last person had finished their tea, they said goodbye and thanked the chef for her generosity. The only one still left at the table was the Little Buddha.

'That was a great meal in wonderful company. Now I understand what you meant when you said sharing makes you happy.'

The old woman's eyes sparkled.

'There's nothing more beautiful to me than these moments of shared joy. No effort is too big if it helps me spend time with old and new friends. To experience life together, that's what it's all about. To laugh and cry and dance and dream together. '

The Little Buddha felt deeply touched. For him it was also important to be alone regularly – but no matter how precious the time in solitude was, it was no substitute for the happiness he felt when he shared special moments with others.

*

The Little Buddha stayed on the bench in front of the house a little longer, then said goodbye too. With slow steps he walked towards the setting sun, thinking about his encounter with the chef. Through her generous actions she fed not only the hungry bellies but also the hearts of her guests. And so, without saying it, she had shown him what really matters: love doesn't exist so that we think, talk and write about it – no, it has to be lived!

Chapter 13
An Unexpected Visit

wo days later the Little Buddha was back home again. He would have arrived even sooner but he got lost on the last leg of his journey, making him wonder how it was possible to know the distant parts of the country better than the area in which he lived.

When he finally stood in front of his big old Bodhi tree again, he was so delighted his eyes filled with tears. He was happy and grateful for everything he had experienced while travelling, but returning home was just as beautiful.

*

Soon after his arrival he was visited by the sad man whose desperate search for a woman had been the reason the Little Buddha had set off in the first place. Full of hope, the man sat down in front of him.

'So, what have you learned about love?'

The Little Buddha didn't know where to begin.

'Can you give me some good advice on how to find a woman now?' the man urged impatiently.

It took a while before the Little Buddha broke his silence.

'I think with love it's the same as with happiness: you will only find it once you stop looking for it.'

'How is that supposed to work? How am I supposed to find something if I'm not looking for it?'

'By simply allowing life to happen. This way the process of finding will eventually occur all by itself.'

'But I can't just sit here and wait without doing anything.'

'I didn't mean it like that. Of course, you ought to keep your eyes open – but without constantly expecting that the next woman you meet will be the one you marry. It's important to have dreams, yes, but expectations only cause unnecessary grief. If your expectation, your burning desire, remains unfulfilled, you'll end up disappointed and so your despair will only grow.'

'Does this mean I shouldn't have any desires?'

'You can have desires but don't become overwhelmed by them. If you wish for something and you're looking for it, you're living in the future. And the future is always unknown and never here. You can only find in the present, that's why it's best to spend more time in the now.'

The words of the Little Buddha made sense to the man, but he was still afraid to spend his life alone.

'And what if I don't find a woman in the present either?'

'You could at least give it a try, at the end of the day you have nothing to lose, do you? Besides, you haven't been successful so far – maybe it's time to change something. And the first thing you could do is stop searching.'

Now it was the man who fell silent. He really would have to change something because he couldn't continue like this. He was definitely not happy at the moment.

*

As the sun rose higher and higher, warming the land with its inexhaustible power, the Little Buddha began to tell his visitor about his journey. He talked about all his experiences and the many different faces of love he had encountered: the yearning postman and the woodcutter's wife, the jealous castle owner, the hard-working weaver and the grateful mother, the silent beekeeper, the lonely monk and the generous chef. He also told him the many wonderful stories he had heard – about the worried student who was shocked to see his master carry a woman across the river, about the queen who sent her daughter's admirers into the forest and about the two brothers who filled life with music. He spoke of vast fields and high mountains, of painful feet and healing hands, of fear and trust, of broken hearts and unconditional love. Of letting go, sharing and becoming one.

'But the most important thing I have learned,' he finally said, 'is that you have to fully accept yourself. You have to learn to make peace with the person you are and love yourself. Because if love exists within you it will spread like a wildfire and other people will be attracted by your love.'

The Little Buddha paused for a moment.

'Really it's quite simple: love life and you'll be happy!'

The last traces of sadness disappeared from the man's face.

'You're right! I don't know how to thank you for your words.'

The Little Buddha looked at him timidly. Then he told him what any other Buddha would have told him too.

'Please don't blindly believe what you heard from me. Have your own experiences and find out the truth for yourself.'

*

A while later, the Little Buddha found himself alone under his Bodhi tree again. He took a few deep breaths, then closed his eyes and enjoyed the light breeze gently caressing his skin.

As he sat there peacefully, he suddenly heard footsteps coming closer. It must be the man again, he thought. Perhaps he had forgotten something or had another question. But when he opened his eyes, he was surprised to see a young woman standing before him. She looked roughly the same age as him and she had the most beautiful smile he had ever seen.

Before they even exchanged their first words, the Little Buddha felt a warm and lively tingling in his belly. It was wild and tender at the same time – an indescribable feeling he had never experienced before. For a moment he forgot everything around him and wished time would stop. And then suddenly he realized what was happening to him.

'So this is what it feels like... No wonder people are crazy about falling in love.'

The End

How was the book?
Please post your feedback:
#LittleBuddha

AMMONITE
PRESS

www.ammonitepress.com